Bloom

EverGreen Trilogy Sequel

ABBY FARNSWORTH

World Castle Publishing, LLC
Pensacola, Florida
Copyright © 2023 Abby Farnsworth
Paperback ISBN: 9798891260764
eBook ISBN: 9798891260771
First Edition World Castle Publishing, LLC, October 23, 2023
http://www.worldcastlepublishing.com
Licensing Notes
Cover: Cover Designs by Karen
https://www.cover-designs-by-karen.com
Editor: Karen Fuller

Table of Contents

Dedication

To my Lily lovers, this is for you.

Acknowledgments

Thank you so much to Karen Fuller and World Castle Publishing! You're the reason these stories stay alive. I couldn't do it without you. Thank you to my family, friends, the members of the press, the business owners, and the community leaders who have supported my work. You guys are great! And even though he can't read (because he's a dog), thank you to my baby boy, Zeus, for making me smile every single morning. You're the best boy I could ask for, and my fingers are crossed for many more years together. And a special thank you to Ryann Renae for giving Lily a voice through our song

"As Always, Yours". It was so much fun working on that project, and I hope we partner again in the future! Lastly, thank you to my readers, especially those who have stayed with me every step of the way. This is our ninth journey together! I hope you feel a whole variety of emotions while reading this book, and most importantly, I hope it makes your heart happy.

"When to the sessions of sweet silent
thought
I summon up remembrance of things
past,
I sigh the lack of many a thing I sought,
And with old woes new wail my dear
time's waste:
Then can I drown an eye, unus'd to
flow,
For precious friends hid in death's
dateless night,
And weep afresh love's long since
cancell'd woe,
And moan th' expense of many a
vanish'd sight;
Then can I grieve at grievances
foregone,
And heavily from woe to woe tell o'er
The sad account of fore-bemoaned
moan,
Which I new pay as if not paid before.
But if the while I think on thee, dear

friend,
All losses are restor'd, and sorrows
end."

"Sonnet 30" by William Shakespeare

Prologue

Beth's cries echoed throughout the house as she woke for the third time in two hours. She was a beautiful baby with pretty, strawberry blonde hair and bright blue eyes, but there was rarely a night when she slept more than a few hours at a time. Beth had just turned one year old, but her fussiness hadn't lessened. She was often sick and underweight. Rowan and I didn't know what to do. The doctors told us she was fine, but that clearly wasn't the case.

Rowan sat up in bed, sighing. "I'll get her. Go back to sleep, baby."

I nodded and rolled over onto my

side. Sometimes, I felt like I barely slept at all. My twins, John and Mina, had just started preschool. The days were quiet, but when they came home, the whole house was filled with chaos. Of course, I loved all of them. It was still hard, though. I had become a mother at twenty and was now twenty-five with three children. I loved my husband and my life, but that didn't make any of it easier.

Rowan came back into the room with Beth in his arms. She was still crying but quieter now. He held a bottle and was trying to convince her to drink from it. She hated them. Nothing made her happy other than breastfeeding, but we were trying to wean her off of it. I could only do so much.

He sat beside me and finally convinced Beth to drink from her bottle. I relished in the temporary silence, and he did, too. Rowan was always tired. He was a phenomenal husband, and he always gave one hundred percent. But he was just a man, and running the business full-time, as well as being the father of three children, took all of the energy out of him. Rowan had just recently completed his master's degree. I was incredibly proud of him, but sometimes I wondered if it had sucked all of the happiness out of his life. We rarely ever had time alone, and I felt cut off from my husband. Our love life was suffering.

I watched as he rocked her back and forth, never giving up. He was still so beautiful. His appearance had barely changed at all since the moment I'd met him. Our anniversary was coming up, but Rowan still looked as perfect as he had when we were eighteen. The only difference was his eyes no longer seemed to glow. The energy Rowan had once possessed was all gone. I didn't love him any less, but I did miss the way his smile used to light up a room. Now, it was strained and exhausted, almost forced.

Still, every Friday, he brought me a fresh bouquet of a dozen white roses and some of my favorite chocolate-covered cherries. Rowan never gave up, no matter how exhausted he was. Still, we rarely ever had dates without at least one child tagging along. Rowan's aunt Marie normally kept the twins, but Beth refused to stay with anyone other than the two of us. The one time we had tried to go to dinner alone, Beth had screamed for two whole hours, leaving Marie clueless as to what to do. Now, we took all three of them with us and spent the nights trying to control two preschool twins and a screaming baby.

I wanted so badly to get away. Sometimes, I wished I could just stay in bed all day and disappear into the covers.

But every morning at eight, Rowan left to drop John and Mina off at school and open the bookstore. I spent the day at home with Beth, doing laundry, cooking, and cleaning. It was nice to be able to spend time with my baby, but I craved the days when I used to have adult interaction. I wanted real conversations and actual communication. I rarely ever had time to discuss adult topics with anyone. All I ever heard was crying, kids' movies, and the chatter of my twins.

Rowan let out a long sigh and placed our sleeping baby down in the bassinet beside our bed. We wanted her to learn to sleep in her own room, but often, it was easier to leave her with us. She cried less when we were in the same room. Rowan laid back down and wrapped his arms around me. I cuddled closer against his shoulder, enjoying his familiar scent. This was the only time we were ever alone. During the day, I craved these silent moments. I wanted to be alone with my husband. It hurt my heart that I rarely ever was.

Just as I was beginning to relax, the alarm clock began screeching. Rowan groaned and rolled onto his side to turn it off. It was time to start another long, boring day.

Chapter One
MORNING

Rowan stood cutting strawberries in the kitchen as I pulled Mina's brown waves into a long, tight braid. She stood perfectly still as I clipped the pink bow into her hair. She was a soft-natured girl and always made the mornings easier. I finished buttoning Mina's blue polo dress and handed her a little white sweater. She fastened on her velcro flats and headed toward the kitchen. Rowan had already combed John's hair and had him ready to go. They both sat down to eat buttered toast, strawberries, and banana slices. Rowan always made sure they ate breakfast. He was adamant about its importance. I was glad he could manage cooking in the mornings—I couldn't. They ate their breakfast quickly and grabbed their little backpacks.

As he grabbed his jacket, Rowan leaned in to give me a quick kiss. I tried to hold on to the two seconds he had his arms around me and felt my heart sink as he pulled away. It was hard to watch him leave. I felt so, so alone.

"I love you," he whispered.

I plastered a fake smile on my face. "I love you, too."

He brushed my hair to the side, smiled, and opened the door. The three of them stepped outside into the fresh morning air and walked toward our black crossover. I watched them go and waved as they pulled out of the driveway. When they were gone, I shut the door and started to cry. The tears began to drip down my cheeks, and I let out a little sob.

This had never happened before. It was the first time I had actually broken down in tears since giving birth to Beth. I had been so emotional at her birth, but the next eleven months had left me numb with barely any emotion at all. It was strange for me. I was normally a very sensitive person. It wasn't necessarily bad, just the truth. I felt things so much more deeply than most people and experienced the world with an intensity that others couldn't imagine. But for so long, my emotions had seemed like they were shut off. I didn't know what to think or how I was supposed to manage the emptiness in my chest.

I sank to the floor and began to sob uncontrollably. It felt like such a silly thing to do. I was a happily married woman with a nice house, plenty of money, and overall healthy children.

My life was relatively drama-free, and I had a kind, supportive extended family. There was no reason to be upset aside from my overwhelming loneliness. It consumed me, and I had no idea why. It wasn't logical, and that frustrated me. I liked having answers to things, and when I couldn't discover them, I became agitated.

After several more minutes of crying, I stood on shaking legs and walked to the kitchen. I opened the refrigerator and examined the contents. Rowan had just gone grocery shopping. There were several different types of berries, plenty of yogurt, chicken, beef, vegetables, and a whole shelf full of cheese. On the counter were apples, bananas, and croissants. I felt nauseous at the thought of eating any of it. Since Beth's birth, most foods had repulsed me. I was lucky to eat one meal a day. Rowan didn't know, though.

He always texted me to remind me to eat lunch. Every day, I lied to him and told him I had already eaten. Telling him I wasn't hungry would make him stressed at work, and I didn't want to do that.

Instead of food, I opted for my usual cup of pomegranate tea. It never made me sick. I watched as the teabag drifted around in the hot water, causing it to turn a deep red. It was the one drink, other than coffee, that I never got tired of. When it was cool enough, I took a sip, enjoying its familiar flavor. The sweet taste gave me a little sliver of happiness.

Then, Beth started screaming. I wanted to throw my mug down in anger, but I managed to set it on the table without violence. Slowly, I counted to ten. I never wanted my children to see me upset. It was something I strived to prevent. But some days, I almost lost my mind in front of them. It was worse when

Rowan wasn't home. He calmed me. But when I was home alone with the baby, it all seemed worse.

I walked upstairs to retrieve Beth from the master bedroom. She was still in her onesie from the night before. Rowan had changed her diaper, so that wasn't the problem, and she had eaten only a little while ago. I picked her up and held her close to my chest. Finally, she stopped crying. The pounding sensation in my mind calmed. For a few moments, the world was quiet.

I wrapped her in a swaddle and tied it around my shoulders. Carrying her was the only way to keep her calm. At least that way, I could have some peace. I walked over to the old-fashioned record player on the nightstand, and Debussy began to fill the room with the sweet sound of a piano. It helped keep my mind clear, at least when Beth wasn't crying. Rowan had given me the record player for Christmas, and it reminded me of him. I always had it playing when he was at work.

I grabbed the laundry hamper and walked down the hallway to the washer and dryer. Our make-shift laundry room was really just a large closet. The house had been built before washers and dryers existed, so no one had known where to put them. Still, I was glad they were on the top floor. At least I didn't have to walk up and down the stairs. I stuffed a load of whites into the washer and threw a pod inside.

The doorbell rang, and I sighed. It was probably someone trying to sell something. We had solicitors come by the house all of the time. It got annoying, and sometimes I just wanted to scream at them. Still, I went to answer the door.

I opened it expecting to find a

salesperson but instead saw Athena on the other side.

She gave me a big smile. "Lily, how are you? I made you some cookies."

I took the tray from her hands and stepped aside to allow her in. "I'm okay. Thanks."

Athena came by the house regularly. Rhett worked long hours, and they had just enrolled Luca in an art-focused day program. He was there from nine to noon, so she was free for several hours in the morning. She stopped by the house several times a week, usually with cookies, cake, or something else she had made. After becoming pregnant again, she took a sudden interest in baking. Now, she was eight months along and cooking far more than the three of them could eat. Most of it ended up at our house.

She walked right into the kitchen

and poured a glass of orange juice. I glanced down at my half-full cup of tea and sighed. It was cold.

"Do you want some orange juice?" Athena asked.

The thought made me nauseous. "No, I'm not thirsty."

She shrugged. "I thought you loved orange juice."

I had, but that was before having Beth. Now, it made me sick.

"I'm just not thirsty," I said.

She gave me a skeptical look but decided not to push it. I walked over to the couch, and she followed me. Beth was still strapped to my chest and sound asleep.

"I can't believe you're having another baby," I said. "You already have a toddler."

She raised her eyebrows. "You have three, Lily. I only have Luca, and I want another. You always say there's no such thing as too many babies. Besides, you had Beth when John and Mina were really little."

I couldn't believe I used to think that. It was a stupid thing to say. There was definitely such a thing as too many babies because I was about to go crazy with three. Rowan and I should have stopped at two, but we hadn't known. I had been so stupid to think I could handle another. Maybe some people could manage it, but not me. I was so tired.

"Well, you might change your mind after you have this one," I replied.

She looked slightly shocked at my comment but chose not to say anything other than, "We're going to name him Ari."

I nodded. "Sounds like a nice name."

She raised her eyebrows. "Lily, are you alright? You seem a little...off. I'm not trying to pry, but you are my best friend."

I shrugged. "Just tired. Wait till you have more than one kid."

Athena gave me a sympathetic smile. "I wish I could help. You know, if Beth wouldn't miss you so much, I would keep her for you. You need more sleep."

I looked down at my sleeping baby, wondering why she was so difficult. "I wish you could help, too."

She looked into my eyes. "I really wish I could do something. If there's anything you think of, just let me know."

I nodded. "I know."

We were both silent for a few moments, not sure of what to say. I knew my mood was making it awkward, but I couldn't muster up any cheerfulness. Besides, Athena was basically family.

I didn't have to pretend for her. Then again, I felt like I needed to when I was with my husband.

"Lily," she whispered, "when was the last time you saw a doctor?"

I gave her a questioning glance. "I finished all of my postpartum check-ups, if that's what you mean. I'm fine. The birth was simple, and I was all healed up in six weeks."

She pursed her lips. "I know it's not my place, but maybe you should see a different doctor. You're like a sister to me, Lily. I don't know where I would be in life without you. I just want to see you happy, and I can tell that you're not. I struggled a little after Luca was born, and this sweet woman, Doctor Lett, gave me some medicine. It really helped. I can give you her number."

I shot her an irritated glance. "I'm not crazy, Athena. I would never hurt

Beth, or John or Mina. Rowan doesn't think there's anything wrong with me."

She looked apologetic. "I know you're not crazy, Lily. I don't mean that at all. But still, what harm could seeing a doctor do? If she's able to help, it would be good. If not, then it won't do any harm."

I didn't want to go, but I did respect Athena. Her suggestions mattered to me. If she thought it was a good idea, I should consider it.

I bit my lip and nodded. "Okay, I'll go. But don't tell Rowan, okay? I don't want him to worry."

Athena smiled. "I promise, I won't say a thing. I really think she might be able to help you, Lily. Trust me."

"I still don't think there's anything wrong with me," I said.

"Well, let's let the doctor see," she replied.

Chapter Two
THE DOCTOR

The next day, I drove my little green car to Doctor Lett's office. She was a women's health specialist who focused on postpartum care. Athena hadn't been able to stop praising her, so I decided it was worth a shot. But I was almost sure there was nothing that could come of it. I was just overwhelmed and tired, both completely normal for a young mother.

I arrived at the doctor's office in a navy blue dress, black cardigan, and black Converse. My hair was pulled back into a bun, and I had a little makeup on. It was important to look decent for these types of things. If I went in there looking sloppy, she might think I actually was crazy. Beth looked good, too. She was wearing a little pink dress with white boots and a bow in her hair. We both looked completely healthy.

When I walked inside, I saw a few other women who looked just like me. They were all well-dressed with babies and tired-looking eyes. Other than the soft sounds of classical music, it was quiet. The office was a beautiful space with dark hardwood floors, lavender walls, and cushy white chairs. The space was lit by a variety of lamps, making it the total opposite of the bright fluorescent lights the hospital had. For a doctor's office, it was comfortable.

Carrying Beth in my arms, I walked over to the desk. There was a little old lady with pink glasses and bleach-blond hair sitting behind the window. She looked like she was in her nineties and barely alive. Still, it seemed like she had more energy than me.

She looked up and smiled. "You must be the new girl. Lily, right?"

I nodded. "Yes."

She handed me a clipboard with a pen and a piece of paper. "Just put your information on there. She'll see you soon."

I mustered up a small smile and took the clipboard from her. Sitting down in one of the chairs, I held Beth with one hand and used the other to write. I filled it out quickly and took it back to the old lady at the window.

She took it from me and smiled again. "Thank you, sweetheart."

"Lily Marx?" a nurse called.

I walked toward her, and through the door she held open for me. The nurse led me into another room and motioned for me to sit down on a pink couch. The walls were painted with pictures of purple flowers and multi-colored butterflies. It was so much different than most doctor's offices.

The nurse had long black hair pulled up in a high ponytail, dark skin, and shimmering eyes decorated with silver eyeshadow. She looked kind and very pregnant. Why was everyone around me having a baby? They were all insane.

"Hello, Lily. I'm Allison, and I'm one of Doctor Lett's nurses. I'm going to check your vitals, and then we'll go over your medical history," Allison said.

I nodded. "Okay."

She took my blood pressure, and she asked me to step on the scale. I didn't know what to do with Beth, but Allison took her from me before I could ask. Looking away, I stepped on the scale.

Allison scribbled down the number and handed Beth back to me. Strangely, Beth wasn't crying. I had no idea whether she was nervous or if it was just one of those rare good days, but I was thankful for her silence.

"Alright, let's go this way," Allison said.

She took me down the hallway into another room. This one was painted light pink and had two purple settees. There were two lamps in the room, along with a small crib with stuffed animals and blankets. Again, I was surprised by how different it was.

Allison motioned to the crib, "You can put your baby down if you'd like. It might make it easier to talk."

I nodded and set Beth down in the crib. She grabbed one of the teddy bears and began to pull on its ears. I sat down, crossed my legs, and looked at the nurse.

Sitting across from me, she began to ask her questions. "How many children have you had, Lily?"

"Three," I said, "two twins and a single."

She nodded. "And how old is your youngest?"

"She just turned one," I answered.

Allison looked over at her. "She's beautiful."

I smiled. "Thank you."

She glanced back down at her paper. "Did you have any problems before or after childbirth?"

I shook my head. "I had one miscarriage before getting pregnant with the twins, but other than that, I've never had any issues. I had simple, easy births."

She gave me a sad smile. "I'm sorry about your miscarriage."

"Thank you," I mumbled.

"Have you ever been diagnosed

with any mental health problems or any medical issues I should know about?" Allison asked.

I shook my head. "I'm completely healthy."

She smiled. "I'm glad to hear it. Well, those are all the questions I have. I'll send Doctor Lett on in."

I nodded. "Alright, Thank you."

She smiled again and closed the door behind her. Only a minute later, Doctor Lett walked in. She was beautiful and had long, curly red hair that fell down to her chest. She wore a white blouse, black pants, and sparkly gold heels. Her lips were bright red, and her smile was just as pretty. She wasn't wearing a wedding ring and didn't look like she had any children. For a second, I envied her. But then I remembered Rowan and realized I was wrong.

"Hello Lily, I'm Doctor Lett, but

please call me Laura," she said.

"Hi," I replied.

She sat down opposite me and glanced over at Beth. "Your baby is beautiful."

I looked at Beth, watching as she played. "Yes, she is."

Laura glanced at her notepad. "Allison said you didn't have any physical problems with any of your births. I'm glad to hear it. I am sorry to tell you that you're underweight, though. It says on the form you filled out that you're one-hundred-and-seventy pounds, but that's not the case. You only weigh one-hundred-and-twenty pounds."

I pursed my lips. "I didn't realize I'd lost so much weight. I normally wear loose-fitting clothing."

She looked surprised. "Well, I would definitely like you to work on that. Your pre-baby weight was much higher. It would be good if you could gain at least thirty pounds."

"I thought one-twenty was acceptable?" I asked.

She sighed. "To some male doctors, yes. But I'm not a man, and I know a woman shouldn't weigh less than a normal middle school boy. It's ridiculous to think that, and it hurts a lot of women. I can tell when a woman isn't eating, and Lily, I know that's you. Is there a reason why? It's important that you tell me."

I shook my head. "I'm not hungry."

She glanced back down at her notepad. "Well, we're going to need to change that. If you lose much more weight, I'm going to have to diagnose you with anorexia, but I don't think that's a correct evaluation of the situation."

I stared at her. "I don't have anorexia."

"I know," Laura said.

"So what's wrong with me?" I asked.

"How much time do you spend alone with your baby?" she replied.

"All day," I said.

Laura nodded. "When do you see your husband?"

"When he gets home from work, about eight," I replied.

She gave me a sad smile. "So you don't see each other much?"

I sighed. "He works hard, and I love him for it. But we don't spend much time together."

She nodded. "How have you been in terms of mood?"

I shrugged. "Fine, I guess. Tired and overwhelmed, but I have three children. That's not a strange thing. Most parents are tired."

She scribbled something down. "Have you been significantly more exhausted since having your third child?"

I nodded. "Yes, but that's normal."

"When did you stop working?" Laura asked.

"When I was pregnant with Beth," I replied. "My husband and I thought it would be good for me to stay home with the baby. We own a bookstore. When the twins were little, we kept them there with us. But it was hard. I knew I couldn't keep three kids with me and work. It just made sense at the time."

She nodded. "So now you're at home, and your twins are in school?"

"Yes," I said.

"When do they get home?" she asked.

"My husband picks them up at two and brings them home before he goes back to work," I said. "I really don't know what this has to do with anything."

She just looked back down at her

notepad. "So you keep all three kids between two and eight? That's six hours by yourself. Do you have any help?"

"Sometimes my husband's aunt, Marie, comes over, but she's busy with her new bakery," I replied.

Laura nodded. "Do you have any other family in the area?"

"My parents moved to Florida, so we don't see them much. My husband's cousin, Ginger and her family live here, but she works full-time. Everyone else moved away," I said.

"So you don't have much interaction with adults then?" she asked.

I shrugged. "My best friend, Athena, comes over some mornings. But she has a son and is going to have another baby in a month. She's busy, too. When her husband gets home from work, she likes to be there."

Laura uncrossed her legs, propped

her elbows on her knees, and looked right at me. "Lily, have you bonded with your youngest daughter?"

I pursed my lips. "What do you mean? I spend all day every day with her."

She nodded. "But do you feel emotionally attached? If she disappeared, how would you feel? Would you be sad or relieved?"

I took a moment to genuinely contemplate her question. How would I feel? What would it be like? When it was just Rowan, me, and the twins, life seemed easier. We spent more time together and did things as a family. We had dinner together almost every night, even if it was just eating takeout at the bookstore. I saw my husband so much more. Rowan was happy, and he looked alive. Now, it was different.

I had a baby that cried all the time.

She was always angry, sick, or upset. John and Mina were such good children. Mina was an angel. She was quiet, loved to paint, and was already reading. John was a little louder, but he was a good boy. He was going to be an incredible artist. His sketches of animals and plants were so beautiful. But Beth, she just screamed.

Laura leaned toward me. "Lily?"

I snapped back to the present. "I don't know."

She nodded. "I thought so. Your problem is normal. There is nothing to feel bad about. You're suffering from postpartum depression. I meet women every day who deal with it. Normally, it's noticed much sooner than a year after childbirth, but I'm not surprised they missed it. Many times, unless the mother is violent, it's ignored."

I stared at her in shock. "I don't understand. I'm not crazy."

She smiled. "I know you're not crazy, Lily, but I am going to give you some medication."

I nodded but remained silent.

"I want to see you back here soon, alright?" she asked.

"Okay," I said.

"Good," she replied. "If you can, I think it would be wise for you and your husband to have some quality time alone. I know it's difficult, but you really should tell him how you feel. Your husband sounds like a good man. I'm sure he wants the best for you."

I nodded. "I'll tell him."

She smiled. "Good, I'll walk you out. You can pick up the medicine at the pharmacy."

Chapter Three
HUSBAND

I arrived home with my new medicine about an hour before Rowan dropped the twins off. He gave me a quick kiss, then got back in the car to go back to work. Without thinking, I helped John and Mina with their homework, read them a few stories, and made pasta for dinner. They ate while chattering about some of the kids at school. Sometimes, it was hard to believe how attached they were. I had never seen two preschoolers so closely bonded, but they were twins. After dinner, they went into the living room to play. I watched for a while, smiling as they set up a little kingdom with their dolls and toy soldiers. They were so creative and smart. I loved seeing them play quietly together.

When Rowan got home, he took John and Mina up to their rooms and read each of them a bedtime story. He rocked Beth for a while, then laid her down before coming back to the kitchen to eat. We had dinner in silence. He looked absolutely exhausted, and I didn't have the heart to tell him about what the doctor had said. Maybe tomorrow.

"How was your day?" he asked.

"Normal," I replied. "How was yours?"

He smiled. "Normal."

We ate silently for a few more minutes. It was already dark outside. A few candles lit up the space, but otherwise, it was pitch-black. That was alright. At least he couldn't see the circles under my eyes, or how much of a disaster my hair was, or the formula spilled all over my dress.

"I saw the twins playing together earlier. It was cute," Rowan said.

I nodded. "It was."

He took a bite of bread. "Beth seems to be doing better. She didn't cry as much tonight."

I shrugged. "It was an okay day."

He got up to put both of our plates in the dishwasher. I had barely eaten anything, so he scraped the rest of mine off into the trash. I knew I needed to eat, but I was too anxious.

"Well, I need to shower," he said. "Do you want to come with me?"

I debated for a minute, then shook my head. When I had changed into sweatpants earlier, I had glimpsed my hips. The bones were sticking out, and I looked unhealthy. My stomach was completely flat, and I could almost see my ribs. I didn't want Rowan to know.

"That's alright. I think I'll lay down," I said.

He looked a little disappointed but nodded. "I'll come to bed in a little bit."

After he left to shower, I went upstairs to our room and noticed something on my pillow. It was a new satin nightgown. There was a note that read, "To my loving wife, from your adoring husband."

I almost started to cry. It was a beautiful dark red color with lace around the edges. I slipped my clothes off and pulled it over my head. Luckily, it was loose, so he wouldn't notice my weight loss. I got into bed and pulled the covers up over me. I picked up my newest book and began to read.

A little while later, Rowan came in. He wore only a loose pair of gray shorts that fell low around his waist. I admired his chest, remembering how I'd felt years ago before our wedding. I had loved him then just as much as I loved him now. He was still my remarkably handsome man.

"Thank you for the nightgown," I said. "It's lovely."

He smiled. "Not as much as you, beautiful."

Rowan slid into bed beside me and tucked my head against his shoulder. He smelled of soap and his normal mint toothpaste. I wanted to wrap myself in his arms and never leave. Being with him was when I truly felt happy. But then I remembered the new pill bottle in my underwear drawer and became a little anxious. What if he was disappointed in me? Did it make me a bad wife? I had to be messed up in the head. Was I the reason Beth was such a sad baby?

"What's wrong, love?" Rowan

asked.

I shook my head. "Nothing, I just want to sleep."

He sat up and looked into my eyes. "Did I do something? If I did, tell me so I can make it right. Was it the nightgown? Did you not like it?"

I took his face in my hands. "You're perfect, Rowan. You never do anything wrong. I just miss you. Nothing more than that."

He wrapped me in his arms and threw his leg over mine. "I miss you too, beautiful."

I cuddled in closer to him and let out a long sigh. "I love you so much, Rowan."

"I love you too, Lily," he mumbled. "Always."

Chapter Four
MOTHER

The next day was entirely normal. John and Mina went to school, and then Rowan brought them back home. It was Friday, so I didn't make them do any homework. Instead, they went outside to play. With Rowan being a summer faerie and me earth, the twins had an interesting combination. There was no real genetic reasoning as to why certain faeries were given their gifts, but sometimes it seemed hereditary. In my family, it certainly was. I had strong genes. Mina was an earth faerie, and she absolutely adored nature. She loved spending time outside. I couldn't keep her out of the flower garden. Unlike Rowan, John was a water faerie. Still, he loved playing with his sister. He was becoming especially talented at creating different figures out of raindrops and treating them like puppets. Rowan had installed a small fountain in our backyard so John could play in it. With both of their abilities, the twins had created a beautiful garden filled with flowers and herbs. It was practically bursting with life. I sat outside with Beth in my lap, watching the two of them play.

Beth was, like her aunts, a fire faerie. Marie was one, too. It seemed to run in their family. Her abilities rarely came out, though. Maybe they would when she was older. For the time being, I was just glad she wasn't burning anything down. I had always worried about that. When I had first glimpsed a little flame in her palm, I panicked. But everyone had assured me that not a single fire faerie they knew of had burned their house down as an infant. That was somewhat comforting.

When it started to get dark, I brought the twins back inside. We had chicken for dinner, along with salads and rolls. They weren't picky eaters, which I was glad about. Beth actually drank her bottle without complaint. It was a rare occurrence. I didn't care what miracle had occurred to put her in such a good mood, but I was glad about it.

I had taken my first pill earlier in the day, but I wasn't supposed to notice a difference for about a week. I still hadn't told Rowan. Maybe I could wait until I felt better to tell him. That way, I would be able to make sure the medicine worked before he got all stressed out about it. I didn't want him to panic about anything.

When they were done with dinner, I gave the twins their baths and took them to bed. Rowan was especially late that night. Since tomorrow was Saturday, he would take them to the bookstore with him. They would spend the day together, so I didn't mind putting them to bed without him. I read them each a story and made sure they were both tucked in.

Beth went down easily, too. She had her bottle, sucked her pacifier, and went to sleep. It was incredible. I walked so delicately out of the nursery, taking a ridiculously long amount of time to make sure I didn't wake her. When I finally managed to take a shower with all of the kids in bed, it felt like the best release ever.

I scrubbed my body several times over, washing my skin with different soaps. Then I massaged shampoo into my dark brown hair, making sure each strand was soaked. It felt so nice to be clean. I had never put so much effort into washing my hair before. After the shampoo, I used a plethora of conditioner before rinsing it all away. My skin felt so fresh, so…new. It was calming and altogether pleasant. When I finally got out of the shower, I put moisturizer on my face and lotion all over my body. I pulled my new nightgown on and went to wait for Rowan.

It was eleven before he finally got home. I had finished my book and started a new one when he eventually came to our bedroom. He rarely ever took so long to finish up at the store. It was definitely an odd occurrence.

"What happened?" I asked.

He gave me an icy stare. "I can't believe you didn't tell me, Lily."

I panicked. "Rowan, I was going to–"

"No," he held up his hand, "let me finish. You didn't tell me how you were feeling or that you were on medication. Do you know how terrible I feel? I feel like the worst, most pathetic husband imaginable. I didn't know you were depressed, Lily. How terrible of a man am I? Did you think I wouldn't care? What was running through your mind?"

Tears began to drip down my cheeks. "This has nothing to do with you, Rowan."

He held up a piece of paper. It was my doctor's report. "It has everything to do with me. I would have supported you. But you didn't give me the chance. Now, I look like a heartless man who doesn't care about his wife. I love you more than my own life, Lily! What did I do to make you think I would ever turn away from you?"

I began sobbing. "Rowan, it's not

you. I didn't mean to hurt you. I thought you would think I'm a bad mother...a bad wife."

His eyes held so much hurt. "You know, I would never think that. All I want is you."

I shook my head. "Rowan, I can't keep doing this. I can't...please. I can't."

He pulled me against him as I kept mumbling the same two words over and over again. I cried into his chest, sobbing until I completely fell apart. His strong arms held me against him, never letting go. After a while, he scooped me up the way he had the day we first met and laid me down on the bed. I kept crying as the tears poured from my eyes like a waterfall. He kissed each one away and wrapped a warm blanket around the both of us. I couldn't stop crying.

"You know I could never see you as anything other than perfect, never," he whispered.

I wrapped my arms around his neck and tangled my fingers in his hair. "I don't deserve you. You have no idea how guilty I feel."

He rolled over and pulled me onto his chest. "Lily, you give me a reason to be alive. Without you, I would have no one. There's no place I'd rather be. Please don't ever be afraid of telling me how you feel. I will listen to anything you have to say. But when you don't give me the chance, I feel like a terrible husband. I don't want to be the man who becomes a stranger to his wife. Please, don't do that to me."

I kept crying. "I don't mean to, Rowan. Please don't stop loving me."

He shook his head. "Baby, that couldn't happen. It's not possible. You're the best parts of my soul. Without you, I wouldn't exist. There's nothing, not depression, not death, not anything that could ever make that change."

"I want to be a good mother. I try so hard," I sobbed into his chest.

He slowly ran his hands through my hair. "You are beautiful. You are a good mother. Depression changes nothing. I only wish I had known."

"Not your fault," I mumbled.

He kissed my palm. "Yes, it is, princess. I should have paid more attention. If I had been home more, I would have noticed."

"You have work," I mumbled.

He tilted my head up so I looked directly into his eyes. "Not right now. We're going to take a break from the store. The kids will stay with Marie, and we're going on a trip."

I shook my head. "We can't leave them. Beth will cry the whole time. And the store, we can't just leave it."

He smiled. "It's been seven months since we tried leaving Beth. She might be okay now. And your parents are flying up to take care of the store. Don't worry."

"When did you figure all this out?" I asked.

He kissed my fingers. "Today. That's why I was late."

I nodded. "I'm sorry I made you upset."

He shook his head. "I was too harsh. I'm sorry. I just got so angry with myself. I should know better than to use that tone with you."

I sniffled and reached for a tissue. "Where are we going?"

He wiped my tears away. "Washington."

"The capital?" I asked.

He shook his head. "The state."

I tilted my head to the side. "Why?"

Rowan smiled. "You'll see."

Chapter Five
FLY

"Mommy, why do you have to go away?" Mina asked.

It was the day after Rowan had told me about our trip, and we were dropping the kids off at Marie's. She was excited to keep them for two weeks. Since Rowan's parents had passed away and mine had moved to Florida, she was like a grandmother to the kids. She did a really good job, too. John and Mina loved going to Aunt Marie and Uncle Forest's house.

"Well, Mommy's doctor thought it would be a good idea for me to take a little trip with Daddy. But I promise this summer, we'll all go to the beach with Aunt Ginger and Giselle, okay? We'll have lots of fun," I answered.

She looked a bit skeptical but nodded and gave me a little kiss. I smiled and hugged her. "Be a good girl, okay? I love you so much."

"Yes, mommy," she said before turning around to go play with Marie's new bulldog puppy.

John walked over and gave me a kiss on the cheek. "I love you, mommy."

I wrapped him in my arms. "I love you too, baby. I'll be home soon, okay?"

He nodded and went to follow his sister. Rowan handed Beth to me, and I looked down into her baby-blue eyes. She really was as beautiful as everyone said. But the doctor was right–I hadn't really bonded with her. Maybe that was why she was so sad. If the medicine started to work, maybe I could fix things. I gave her a little kiss and handed her to Marie.

"You two have fun, and don't worry about anything here," Marie said, "we have it all under control."

I gave her a hug. "Thank you."

Rowan took my hand and pulled me away, and I followed him out the door. It was hard leaving the twins. We were going to be gone for two whole weeks. I had never left them alone for more than a weekend before. What if they got sick or broke a bone? I wouldn't be able to get back to them soon enough. But I trusted Rowan's aunt and uncle with my life, so I could trust them with my babies, too.

I got into the passenger seat beside Rowan and buckled my seatbelt. He took my hand in his and smiled. "Are you ready?"

I smiled back. "I guess so."

He laughed. "Don't worry, we'll

have fun. Marie is more than capable of taking care of the kids. Remember, she raised Ginger and Giselle. They turned out fine."

I nodded. "You're right."

He squeezed my hand and pulled out of the driveway.

We drove over an hour to the airport. I had never been on a plane before. Flying scared me. Rowan had flown several times, so he knew what we were supposed to do. Walking through the airport felt like a blur. The whole time, I was anxious and sweating. Rowan kept telling me not to stress. We both knew better than to assume that would happen.

The flight took five hours. At first, all I could focus on was how high up in the air we were. We were flying first class, so it wasn't uncomfortable. Still, I gripped the sides of my seat like I was hanging on for dear life. Rowan did his best not to laugh at me. After a few hours and several cups of Earl Grey tea with extra sugar, I finally relaxed. I pulled out my copy of Pride and Prejudice and distracted myself for the rest of the flight.

Chapter Six
RAIN

When we finally arrived, it was eight o'clock at night and completely dark outside. The rain was pouring down, and clouds covered the sky. It was stereotypical Washington weather. I wasn't exactly sure why Rowan had selected this location, but it was very different from home. Maybe that was the goal.

We left the airport and called a taxi to take us to wherever Rowan had booked for our stay. I had no clue where we were going. The taxi ride took at least an hour. I was surprised the driver had agreed to take us. He was an older man with graying hair and a long beard. His voice was low and loud, but he seemed friendly enough. Rowan talked to him the whole time about the weather they normally had. I just stayed quiet, glad I didn't have to talk.

Finally, we drove off onto a side road with lots of potholes. The car bumped up and down as we traveled down the road. With the rain pouring so heavily, I was surprised the driver could see anything. But he seemed to know where we were going, which was a relief.

Eventually, he pulled into a driveway that went up a little hill. After a bit, we reached a small log cabin with a cute front porch and lanterns hanging near the front door. The windows were covered by green shutters that were decorated with a pretty floral design. Overall, it was a very quaint house.

Rowan helped me out of the cab and grabbed our bags from the back. The driver waved as he drove away. Rowan, being far friendlier than me, waved back.

"This way, baby," he said as he led me up the porch stairs.

The house was already unlocked, so we went right in. It was a beautiful space with a hardwood floor, leather furniture, a glowing fireplace, lit candles, and a cottage-core feel. The kitchen was filled with dark green cabinets, a basket of fruit, and a well-stocked fridge.

"Where did all this food come from?" I asked.

Rowan smiled as he set our bags down. "I had the owners stock it for us."

There were berries, cheese, and plenty of eggs. My favorite green juice sat on the top shelf, along with a fresh container of cold brew. There was also a whole rotisserie chicken and homemade potato salad.

I kept exploring the house and found a large bathroom with a clawfoot tub, a big shower, and a variety of new lotions and perfumes. The bedroom was huge, with a king-size bed covered by a cozy quilt, two nightstands with stacks of books, and a beautiful wooden chandelier.

It was a perfect little house. Rowan had known exactly the most romantic place to rent. I couldn't imagine a better location for a second honeymoon.

I gave him a light kiss. "This is perfect, Rowan."

He wrapped his arms around me. "I'm glad you think so. I kept searching for the right place. This seemed like exactly what I was looking for."

"What do you want to do?" I asked.

He pulled me in for a long, slow kiss. "How about a bath?"

I nodded. "That sounds good."

"I'll go get the water ready," he said.

As he walked away, I looked out the large window facing the woods. It was still pouring outside. The cabin was warm and comfortable, but the surrounding forests were chilly and damp. I shivered at the thought of being outside. It was beautiful, yes. But I could have never lived in Washington. I enjoyed the sun. There was something magical about this place, but it was also dreary. I understood that. The weather seemed appropriate, considering my mood.

Rowan came up behind me and wrapped his arms around my waist. "The water is ready."

I leaned against him. "Sounds good."

He placed gentle kisses along the top of my head. "You're so gorgeous."

I looked up into his beautiful brown eyes. "I feel like a mess."

He smiled sadly and brushed my long hair to the side. "I know, love. But I'm going to try to change that. A few weeks of adult-only time will do you good. No diapers to change or midnight feeding sessions. It'll be relaxing."

I placed my head on his shoulder. "You're right, it'll be good."

"I know, love," Rowan whispered.

Chapter Seven
GIVE UP

I sat on the counter as Rowan dried each individual strand of my hair. He was very focused. His was still a wet mess of curls, but he was determined to dry every inch of mine. My hair had grown back to its former length. It fell down to my waist in long, straight strands of chocolate. I had always found my hair so flat and boring, but Rowan loved it. After having the twins, I had chopped it off to shoulder length, and it had been nice for a while. But then I had started missing my old hair and spent the next few years growing it out.

"This is taking forever," I grumbled.

"Don't you do this every day?" Rowan asked.

I raised my eyebrows. "You have to be kidding."

He looked at me in confusion. "No, I thought women usually dried their hair."

I laughed. "Maybe childless ones. It's hard to find an hour of spare time to dry my hair."

Rowan nodded. "I guess I never thought of that."

I shrugged. "It's alright. I don't usually mind."

He paused and turned the hairdryer off. "What else do you give up?"

I looked directly into his eyes. "What do you mean?"

"Since having Beth, what else have you had to stop doing?" he asked.

"Well, lots of things," I said. "I

don't normally have any time to go to the bathroom alone or eat in peace. When I shower, I have to do it in less than five minutes, or else one of them will interrupt me. I do a lot more laundry, and I'm always finding dirty plates around the house. There are candy wrappers everywhere, and cookie crumbles all over the couch. I clean most of it before you get home."

He pursed his lips. "I didn't realize. I'm sorry."

I reached up to cup his face. "It's alright. You work long hours. I don't want you to be stressed about all of that when you get home."

Rowan frowned. "Still, it's not fair to you."

"It's okay," I said. "Maybe when they get older, I'll have more free time."

"I feel like I don't help you with anything," he replied.

I shook my head. "Rowan, you leave the house early every single morning and don't get to come home until eight. I couldn't ask you to do any more than that."

He sighed. "I still feel bad."

I smiled. "It's okay. I just wish we had more time together."

He nodded. "I do, too."

"Come on," I said, "let's go to bed."

I put on a pair of comfy sweatpants and one of Rowan's big hoodies. There was a TV under the bed that I hadn't noticed before, and Rowan pulled it out so we could watch a movie. There was a large selection in one of the cabinets, and I started scanning for something good to watch. There were lots of boring-looking documentaries and a few action movies I definitely didn't want to watch. But then I noticed something perfect–my favorite movie of all time. I pulled out the 1995 version of Sense and Sensibility with Kate Winslet and Alan Rickman. They were my two favorite actors, starring in the best movie ever made. I grabbed it off the shelf and headed back to bed.

Rowan was already lying down under a fuzzy blanket. I stuck the DVD inside the TV and crawled in beside him. It had been so long since I'd watched it. Normally, cartoons were always playing in our house. The kids loved Disney movies, so we were always watching something to do with a princess or superhero. I didn't mind, but it was nice to finally watch a movie that wasn't meant for preschoolers.

Rowan smiled. "You found it."

"What do you mean?" I asked. "You knew it was here?"

He grinned. "I asked the owners to leave us a few of your favorite movies. Thought it would be fun to watch you discover them."

I rolled my eyes. "You're ridiculous."

He laughed. "You love it."

As the movie began to play, he handed me a bowl of M&M's and a cup of hot chocolate. Rowan really was perfect. Sometimes, I still wondered if he was real. He had never ceased to be everything I'd ever dreamed of having. Rowan was steady, much more than I ever would be. He was levelheaded but not boring. I didn't have to worry about him running away, but I wasn't concerned about him becoming a cranky old man, either. He was the perfect in-between. Rowan had never lost his charm. I was still so in love with him, and that would never change.

I cuddled up against my husband as he leaned over to turn the lamp off. Other than the light from the TV, it was completely dark. The soft patter of rain falling on the roof sounded all around us. It was cathartic. Rowan wrapped his arm around me and laid his head against mine. I never felt safer than when I was beside him.

The movie continued to play, and I started to doze off. The last thing I heard was Kate Winslet say, "Is there any felicity in the world superior to this?" and then the familiar reply, "I told you it would rain." After that, I closed my eyes and fell asleep in my husband's arms.

Chapter Eight
MAKE SURE YOU KNOW

I woke the next morning with Rowan's arm wrapped around my chest and his leg thrown over mine. He was sound asleep, and his breathing was slow, deep, and steady. For a few minutes, I just stayed still and listened to the sound of his heartbeat. I pressed my ear against his chest. It was one of the most beautiful sounds in the world.

"Mmm, good morning," he whispered.

"Morning," I mumbled.

"How'd you sleep?" he asked.

I stretched my arms out above my

head. "Good, you?"

He yawned. "Good."

I grabbed my robe from the hook on the back of the door and headed toward the kitchen. Slowly and methodically, I made a pot of coffee. Rowan followed me out and wrapped his arms around my waist.

"I love you," he mumbled.

"I love you too, babe," I whispered.

He gave me a soft kiss and turned to open the fridge. Rowan pulled out a variety of fruit and started washing it off. He grabbed two bowls from the cabinet and began to fill them. It was nice to just be around him. I liked feeling his presence near mine, our shoulders brushing as we moved past each other. There was something so simple yet so nice about it. Being close to Rowan was like coming home after a long trip away. It was calming.

"What are we doing today?" I asked.

He handed me a bowl. "Well, I picked out a trail for us to go up the mountain. There's a nice view. It's not supposed to rain, so it should be beautiful."

I poured him a mug. "Sounds good to me."

He smiled. "Let's finish up breakfast, and then we can get dressed."

I nodded and began to sip my coffee.

When we finished eating, and I'd had three cups of coffee, I drank some juice and got dressed. For the first time in a while, I'd actually eaten a full, healthy meal. I felt good, even rejuvenated. I had never been a morning person, but having the opportunity to spend time alone with Rowan gave me a lot of energy.

I pulled my hair into a long braid

that fell down my right side down to my waist. After getting everything out of my bags, I chose a pair of leggings, a hoodie, and tall socks with duck boots. Even though it was spring, it was still chilly outside. Washington wasn't ever a warm place. I was used to nicer weather. It would be okay, though. If Rowan wanted to hike up into the woods, then I would go. Anything to be close to him.

Rowan stuffed two water bottles and some granola bars into a small backpack. He strapped it on and held out his hand. I took it in mine.

"Ready?" he asked.

"Oh, as ready as I usually am for hiking," I said.

He laughed. "Don't worry, I won't let you fall. The idea of carrying you for over a mile doesn't sound particularly appealing. No offense, love."

I rolled my eyes. "Uh-huh."

He pulled me against his chest. "I promise you'll enjoy it."

I smiled. "I believe you."

He gave me a tender kiss. "Good, baby."

We walked uphill for a full half hour before I had to stop. We rested on a rock for a few minutes while I drank some water. It was maybe forty degrees out. If we hadn't been walking for so long, I would have been cold. I was sweating; Rowan wasn't. We kept going further and further up the hill. Part of me wanted to turn back, but I didn't want to ruin his fun. He seemed like he was having a great time. At one point, I tripped in the mud and almost fell face-first onto a sharp rock. Rowan caught me, though, so I didn't even get my leggings dirty.

"Close call," he mumbled.

I nodded, completely out of breath. "Uh-huh."

It felt like forever until we finally reached the top of the mountain. When we made it, I let out a sigh of relief. Rowan was right. It was beautiful. I could see out into the blue sky, watching as birds flapped their wings and soared around the clouds. There were thousands of evergreen trees all around. Everything was so vibrant. I took it all in, basking in Mother Nature's beauty. It was an incredible landscape.

Rowan smiled. "Beautiful, isn't it?"

I nodded. "It's stunning."

He wrapped his arm around my back. "Not as much as you, baby."

I laughed. "Thanks, but I think you're lying. You always say that even when I look like a mess. Case in point, right now."

He shook his head. "I never have to lie, not about your beauty."

"Thank you," I whispered.

"Of course," he said.

We stood for a few more minutes in silence before he reached into his back pocket. I barely paid attention, assuming he was reaching for another snack. But when he got down on one knee in the mud, I looked at him in shock.

He smiled as he opened the little black box. There was a beautiful diamond ring inside with small emeralds all around it. I couldn't imagine any piece of jewelry being more elegant. It looked as if it belonged on the finger of a queen, certainly not me.

"Lily Marx, will you marry me again?" he asked.

I laughed. "Yes, I'll marry you again."

He slipped the ring on the other ring finger, the one that didn't have my wedding band on it, and pressed his lips against mine. It was a needy kiss, the kind we hadn't had in a long time. It reminded me of when we were first married, still so young. But we were only twenty-five, and in the story of our lives, that really wasn't very old. I had never imagined that he would want to marry me again. We were approaching our wedding anniversary, and everything seemed so busy. Our lives were filled with so much stress. We barely ever saw each other. But still, he wanted me to commit to being his wife again. The thought made me smile. Rowan was still as sweet as ever. It reminded me of why I had fallen in love with him in the first place. He made my life magical in every way. One day, when we were old, I would look back on this fondly. It would remind me of how much my husband loved me.

"Thank you," I whispered. "I really needed this."

He smiled. "I know, baby. You

deserve so much. I need to make sure you know how important you are to me. There's no one in the world I love more. You're my universe. Without you, I wouldn't know what to do with myself. You have given me three beautiful children and eight amazing years of pure, unconditional love. There's nothing I could ever do to truly show how much that means to me. But at least this ring, and reaffirming our vows, will help remind you that meeting you was the best thing that ever happened to me."

I wrapped my arms around his neck. "I'm so glad you're my husband."

He pulled me tight against his chest. "And I'm so glad you're my wife."

We stood there for a long time, just listening to the sound of each other breathing. He didn't mind holding me, and I relished being held. His arms were paradise. He was my reason for staying alive and the man who had truly shown me what love was. Rowan Marx was the best man I had ever met, and he was mine.

Chapter Nine
BREATHING

Later that night, I made ham sandwiches with lettuce, tomato, and mayo for dinner. Rowan baked fresh brownies and opened a bottle of wine. We sat in bed eating and watching the 1939 version of Wuthering Heights. Rowan knew it was also one of my favorites. I enjoyed black and white films. There was something so simple about them. Even though I obviously hadn't been alive when they were popular, I felt nostalgia for them. Black and White movies were timeless and so romantic. Years ago, when I was sixteen, I had done a report on this version of Wuthering Heights. I was still proud of the fact that I had gotten the best grade in the class. I certainly didn't miss high school, but there were a few things I had enjoyed.

When Rowan's phone started to ring, I paused the movie. No one had called us the whole time we were away. Marie had sent me a few pictures of the kids playing, but other than a couple texts, I hadn't heard anything. Rowan answered the phone.

"Hey, is everything okay?" he asked.

I heard a panicked voice on the other end.

Rowan put it on speaker. "Okay, Marie, calm down and explain to me what happened."

She sounded terrified. "Beth stopped breathing when she was asleep. I went to check on her while the twins were playing, and she had turned this terrible blue color. I panicked. I had never seen a baby turn that color before. Forest wasn't home, and I had no idea what to do. I called an ambulance, and we're at the hospital now."

I heard myself gasp. "Is she okay?"

Marie took a deep breath. "She's breathing again, but the doctors are keeping her here. You need to come home."

"Where are the twins?" Rowan asked.

"They're with Ginger," she said, "Giselle is flying up from Jacksonville to help. Forest and Drew are with her now. I'm here at the hospital alone."

"Okay, we'll head to the airport," Rowan said.

"Oh, there's one more thing you should know," Marie said. "When Ginger texted Athena, she was in so much shock that she went into labor. Rhett just brought her to the hospital. The baby is coming early. Luca is staying with Ginger, too."

Rowan nodded. "Okay, thanks. We're coming."

He hung up the phone and looked at me. "Lily, it's going to be alright."

I felt lightheaded. "She stopped breathing…why did she stop breathing?! What happened?!"

"I don't know," he answered, "but we're going to find out. Marie will keep us updated. I'm going to call a cab, and we'll get the first flight home."

"What if…," I whispered.

"No," Rowan said, "that's not going to happen. Beth is at the hospital, and there are plenty of doctors taking care of her. She's going to be fine."

I nodded. "Okay."

He got off the bed and called the

cab. I started throwing our clothes back into our bags and hurriedly threw our half-eaten food away. Our wine glasses remained barely touched. I was so panicked that my hands were shaking. I could barely manage to breathe. If I hadn't had so much adrenaline pumping through my veins, I wouldn't have been able to stand. All I could feel was fear. My baby had stopped breathing. My sweet little girl was in the hospital, and I hadn't been there for her. She was probably terrified. What if something happened before we got home? I would never forgive myself. She couldn't die. It just couldn't happen.

As soon as the cab arrived, I sprinted out of the cabin with my new ring on my finger. Rowan threw our bags in the back and told the driver to go as fast as we could. The whole time, I felt like I was separated from my body.

I could hear my own heart pounding. Rowan's hands were squeezed into fists, and even he looked scared. We had never expected this. John and Mina had always been healthy. I had never had any complications when I was pregnant with Beth. She had always been fragile, but nothing like this. The doctors had told me she was fine. They had been wrong. If Marie hadn't noticed, Beth could have died in her crib. We were lucky she was still alive. But I still couldn't bear the thought of her being in the hospital.

As soon as we got to the airport, Rowan explained the situation to the lady at the front desk and got us two first-class tickets on a plane that was going back home in five minutes. I had never felt so helpless before. There was nothing for me to do until I got back. Until we landed at home, I wouldn't be able to help my baby. It made me feel like the most terrible mother in the world.

Chapter Ten
SURGERY

As soon as we arrived at the hospital,
I rushed to the ICU. Rowan was right
behind me. When we reached the floor,
Marie met us with tears in her eyes. She
wrapped me in her arms and started
sobbing.

"I'm so sorry, Lily," she cried.

"Shh, it's not your fault," I said.

"Where is she?" Rowan asked.

A tall male doctor stepped out from
behind Marie. He had a confident but
sympathetic expression on his face. The
anxiety in his eyes made me nervous. He
looked young, maybe thirty. Hopefully,

he knew what he was doing.

"Your daughter is in surgery, sir," he said.

Panic crossed my face. "What's wrong with her?"

He looked down at me. "She has congestive heart failure, Mrs. Marx."

Rowan's jaw dropped. "She's in open-heart surgery?"

I felt like the whole world was spinning. Everything seemed fuzzy. I gripped Rowan's arm, and he leaned down to support me.

"Yes, sir," the doctor said, "I'm Doctor Lewis. I saw Beth as soon as she arrived. The EMTs got her breathing again, and I ran some tests. As soon as we found out her condition, she went straight to the operating room with our best pediatric surgeon."

I looked at him in desperation. "Is she going to be okay?"

He nodded. "It's looking good. I think she'll be just fine. Beth will need to stay on some medication and, of course, come back for follow-up appointments, but the surgery has gone perfectly so far."

I let out a long sigh of relief. "When can I see her?"

"A few hours," he replied. "As soon as she's out of surgery, I'll let you know."

Rowan nodded. "Thank you, we'll be waiting."

The doctor gave us a tight smile and walked away. Rowan wrapped his arm around my waist and helped me to a chair. Marie sat down beside me and took my hand in hers.

A smiling nurse with a head-full of blond curls walked over to us. She wore dark pink scrubs and shiny purple shoes. "Is there anything I can get you?"

"Some water?" I asked.

She nodded. "Of course." The nurse came back with two cups and handed one to me and the other to Marie. "I promise, the lead pediatric surgeon here is very skilled. He's done plenty of these surgeries before on children even younger than Beth. She'll be fine."

I took a drink of water. "Thank you."

"What's your success rate?" Rowan asked.

She smiled. "Ninety-five percent."

I felt a little relieved. That was good. My baby would be okay. I just wanted her safe in my arms. Nothing else seemed to matter. All I cared about was her surviving. Rowan gripped my shoulder tightly. I could tell from how strongly he squeezed that he was nervous, too.

The nurse nodded. "Well, if you need anything else, let me know."

"Thank you," I said.

"How's Athena?" Rowan asked Marie.

She smiled. "The delivery went well, and Ari is a beautiful, healthy boy."

I sighed. "Good. I feel horrible that she went into labor because of this."

Marie squeezed my hand. "It's alright. Ari is already six pounds. Looks just like his mother. He doesn't even have to go to the NICU. They'll take him home tomorrow morning."

Rowan nodded. "Good. We'll send some flowers."

Marie nodded. "I just hope Beth is alright."

I closed my eyes and took a deep breath. "Me too."

"What did you tell the twins?" Rowan asked.

"Forest hasn't told them much of anything. Ginger is keeping them distracted. Giselle just got here. They're going to bring all of the kids to the hospital when they bring Luca to come visit his brother," she said.

"Can they stay with you tonight?" Rowan asked. "Lily and I will probably stay here with Beth."

Marie nodded. "Of course."

The ICU doors swung open as my childhood best friend, Jack, walked in with his wife, LeAnne, right behind him. I stared at them in shock. No one had told me they were coming.

"Jack?" I whispered.

"Lils," he mumbled as he wrapped me in his arms, "How's baby Beth?"

I sniffled. "She's in surgery. Who told you?"

"Rowan texted me," he said. "We got on a plane as soon as we could. Will she be alright? What's wrong with her?"

"She has congestive heart failure,"

I mumbled.

Shock crossed his face. "Can they help her?"

"They're operating on her heart right now," Rowan said.

LeAnne looked down at me with sympathy. "I'm so sorry, Lily."

"Thanks," I whispered.

"Is there anything we can do?" Jack asked.

Silent tears started dripping down my cheeks. It was all starting to register. I was still in shock, but when that went away, I was going to explode.

"I don't know," I whispered.

He nodded. "Well, LeAnne can go get us a hotel room, and I'll stay here."

"Oh no, don't get a hotel room. I'll give you the spare keys to our house," Rowan said.

LeAnne took the keys. "Thanks. Do you want me to bring you anything?"

Rowan smiled. "I'll text you."

Jack stood up. "I'll get you some candy from a vending machine. There has to be one here. What do you want?"

"I don't know anything," I said.

He gave me a sad smile. "I'll get something sweet. Be right back, Lils."

Chapter Eleven
ALRIGHT

We waited for four more hours before hearing any more news about Beth. LeAnne brought me several books from the house, but I couldn't read. After giving me a kiss on the cheek, Marie left to put the twins to bed. Jack sat beside me, staring off into space while biting his lip, and Rowan was pacing the waiting room floor. All I was able to do was scroll through newborn pictures of Beth on my phone. We'd had a photo shoot just a week after her birth and dressed her up in lots of pretty outfits. I couldn't stop staring into her gorgeous blue eyes.

They were so innocent and filled with life. She looked like a little angel. I truly loved her more than my own life. The prospect of losing her had kicked my motherly instincts into high gear. It no longer mattered that I had Postpartum Depression and hadn't really bonded with her. She was still my baby. I wished I could have been in there instead of her. I would have given my life for any of my children. The knowledge that I couldn't do anything made the wait seem to last forever. Beth had so much life left to live.

Finally, the nurse came back. "Beth is out of surgery. Everything went well. If you come with me, I'll take you back to her."

I had never been so happy in my life. "So she's okay?"

The nurse smiled. "Yes, she's okay."

Jack and Rowan both looked

relieved. We followed the nurse hurriedly back to Beth's room. Doctor Lewis and another man were already there. I ran over to Beth's crib and looked down at her. She had all kinds of wires and tubes attached to her body, but she was breathing. Her skin was back to its normal paleness, and everything seemed alright.

Doctor Lewis motioned toward the other man. "This is Doctor Cole. He operated on your daughter. He wanted to talk to you in person."

Rowan shook his hand. "Thank you so much."

Doctor Cole smiled. "Of course. I was a little worried at first, but everything went fine. Your daughter will need to stay at the hospital for a week. But after that, as long as you give her the medication I'm prescribing, she'll be alright."

I reached down to touch her. They

kept talking, but I didn't listen. Rowan was asking about the specifics of the procedure, but all I could do was look at my baby girl. Jack stood beside me, staring at all of the wires.

"At least she's okay," he whispered.

I nodded. "She's alive."

The two doctors left, and Rowan came to stand on my other side. He reached down and touched her cheek. It was so sad to see her with all the wires and tubes. I hated that my baby had been an inch away from death, and I hadn't even been able to help her. But the doctors were certain she would live. I felt more relief than I could possibly put into words. My baby wasn't going to die. Everything else seemed less important than it once had.

"She's going to be okay, baby," Rowan whispered as he wrapped his arm around me.

I nodded. "I know."

We silently watched her breath for several more moments. She was the most beautiful baby in the world. I heard the methodical beep of the machines and the noise outside the door, but everything in the world seemed to fade away as I watched her chest rise and fall. Her heart was beating. My little girl was going to grow up to be happy and healthy. I was going to bond with her and make sure she got all the love she needed. Nothing would ever tear me away from her again. It felt like a huge weight had been lifted off my chest. I could feel deeply again. My love for Beth no longer seemed muffled by sadness. Now, it was all raw and open. I leaned against Rowan as we continued to stare down at our baby girl.

"That was a close call," Jack whispered.

I wiped a tear away and laughed.

"A little too close for me."

Rowan nodded. "But she'll be alright."

I smiled. "Yes, and so will we."

Chapter Twelve
UNCONDITIONAL

I sat beside Beth. There were two chairs in the room. Rowan slept in one while I sat in the other. I had tried to fall asleep several times, but I couldn't. Rowan wanted to be awake, but he couldn't keep his eyes open. I didn't blame him. I had already had five cups of coffee and was now sticking to espresso.

It was just impossible for me to look away from her. She was still breathing steadily, but I didn't want to leave her side. I was terrified that if I got up, she would stop breathing again. For some reason, watching her made me feel better.

"You're gonna be okay," I whispered.

I wasn't sure whether or not she could hear me, but maybe she could feel my presence. I didn't want her to be scared. She must have felt so alone. At least she wouldn't remember it. It would be stuck in my mind forever, but when she was older, she would have no memory. I was glad. It was hard enough now.

I stroked her curls out of her face. "I'll love you forever, princess. Mommy will never stop loving you."

She was so beautiful. Her long black eyelashes fluttered every couple of seconds. She seemed to be sleeping peacefully. I wondered what she was dreaming about. Maybe butterflies–she loved those. Jack had brought a few of her stuffed animals from home: a teddy bear, a puppy, and a kitten. They hadn't let me put a blanket on her, but I'd pulled some socks on her feet to make sure she was warm. Still, I worried she'd get cold or uncomfortable. I was constantly panicking about everything. It was hard to relax.

I rummaged through the bag of books LeAnne had brought me for something to read out loud. Maybe Beth would like that. The nurse said it was good for her to hear me talking and that my voice would make her feel better. I hoped that was true.

I pulled my copy of Shakespeare's Sonnets out of the bag and began to read.

"Shall I compare thee to a summer's day?
Thou art more lovely and more temperate:
Rough winds do shake the darling buds of May,

And summer's lease hath all too short a
date;
Sometime too hot the eye of heaven
shines,
And often is his gold complexion
dimm'd;
And every fair from fair sometime
declines,
By chance or nature's changing course
untrimm'd;
But thy eternal summer shall not fade,
Nor lose possession of that fair thou
ow'st;
Nor shall death brag thou wander'st in
his shade,
When in eternal lines to time thou
grow'st:
So long as men can breathe or eyes can
see,
So long lives this, and this gives life to
thee."

-Shakespeare Sonnet 18

Rowan woke halfway through my reading and stared at me with a smile on his face. His eyes held so much pure, unconditional love. Even after years and years together, I still felt my heart speed up when he looked at me.

"I love listening to your voice," he murmured.

I blushed. "Well, thank you."

He smiled. "You're so beautiful when your cheeks turn pink. I love it, baby."

Rowan was so sweet. "You think too much of me," I whispered.

"Absolutely not, baby," he said. "I only see what you can't. I see my beautiful wife, the mother of my children, and my partner for as long as I live and in whatever life comes after this one. You're everything to me."

"You're too good for me, Rowan,"
I whispered.

He shook his head. "Oh baby,
you're too good for me."

I watched as he walked across the
room and knelt down in front of me. He
took my hand in his and admired my
new ring. It sparkled in the hospital light.

"This ring looks so good on your
finger," he said.

I smiled. "It's far too beautiful for
me."

Without saying anything, he leaned
over and pulled me into a gentle kiss. I
relished in the taste of him and allowed
everything else to fade away. He was the
love of my life, and I could never forget
that. We had been together for years and
had three children together, but he still
surprised me with his overwhelming
love. There was never a day when he
didn't show me how much I meant to

him. That was what kept me motivated in life.

"I love you so much," I whispered.

He smiled. "I love you too, baby. Thank you for being mine."

I pulled him back for another tender kiss. "And thank you for being mine."

Beth let out a gentle cry, and we both jumped up to be at her side. She looked almost normal. A nurse walked in with a bottle in hand. She had a smile on her face.

"Don't worry, she's okay, just hungry. Would you like to be the one to feed her?" she asked.

I nodded. "Of course. Can I pick her up?"

The nurse smiled. "Yep, just be careful of the cords. We need to keep monitoring her."

I slowly picked Beth up and cradled her against my chest. She stopped crying, nuzzling her head into my neck. I took a long, deep breath. My baby was breathing in my arms. She had enough strength to cry, and I was going to feed her. I took the bottle from the nurse. She walked out and left Rowan and me alone with our baby.

Beth instantly reached for the bottle and began sucking on it. She gulped it down quicker than ever before. I was amazed at her strength. For such a small baby, I had expected it to take far longer for her to recover. But she was alright, and I was so thankful for that.

Doctor Lewis walked in with a smile on his face. "How's the patient?"

Rowan smiled back. "She's doing well, just gulped down a whole bottle."

"That's good news," Doctor Lewis said, "she's recovering faster than I expected."

"Thank you so much for taking

such good care of her," I replied.

He nodded. "That's my job, ma'am. It's always hard with the children. I have to say, I'm a bleeding heart. But your daughter was determined to live. She's going to be a feisty one when she's older."

Rowan laughed. "I can imagine. She's very similar to certain members of our family."

I grinned. "Oh yes, just like her aunts."

Doctor Lewis smiled. "I'm glad to know Beth has such a supportive family. She may end up needing more medical intervention in the future. I'm not sure. For now, she looks good, but things change. She'll need your support."

Rowan nodded. "We'll do everything we can."

"I know," Doctor Lewis said, and walked out the door.

Chapter Thirteen
BEAUTIFUL BABY

One week later, we brought Beth home from the hospital. She would need about another month to fully heal. Until then, I was determined not to leave her side. My parents were staying in town to help Rowan run the bookstore so he could spend more time at home with us. Even John and Mina understood that Beth was sick. John avoided her, afraid she might break if he touched her. Mina sat with Beth a lot and sang lullabies to help her sleep. I loved seeing them so peaceful together. It warmed my heart. I loved them more than I had once known was possible.

"We're here!" Athena announced as she opened the front door, followed by her oldest son, Luca, and husband, Rhett, who was carrying their baby.

I smiled and gave her a big hug. "How are you?"

She shrugged. "I feel great. It wasn't nearly as hard as Luca's birth. Ari is perfectly healthy and a quiet baby. I couldn't ask for more."

I held out my arms. "Can I hold him?"

Rhett nodded. "Of course."

I took little Ari in my arms and gazed down into his blue eyes. He really did look like his mother. Ari was indeed a beautiful baby. Athena and Rhett were both glowing with joy. Luca seemed a little skeptical about the whole thing, but he was also interested. John had reacted the same way to Beth's birth.

"He's beautiful," I said.

Athena smiled. "Thank you. He's the final member of our family. Everything feels complete now."

"I'm glad," I said, "we're very happy for you."

"Can I hold him?" Mina asked.

Athena smiled at her. "Sure, let's go sit on the couch, and I'll hold him with you."

I handed Athena her baby and watched as Mina sat on the couch. When Athena softly placed Ari in Mina's arms, she looked down at him with amazement. Mina was so nurturing. She was definitely an empath. I loved that about her. Mina's softness was her strength.

Rowan carried Beth into the room. Rhett looked at him. "How is she?"

"She's doing great," Rowan said. "I'm relieved. It was the scariest thing I've ever experienced. And all things considered, that means a lot."

Rhett nodded. "I can't imagine how it must have been for you. We were all terrified for her. I'm glad she's doing well."

I let out a long sigh. "It's been a rough week for everyone."

The door opened, and Giselle burst into the room. Her bouncing red curls followed her like a wave of fire. She had a huge smile on her face as she ran right over and wrapped her arms around me. Ginger, Drew, and Gracie, their daughter, followed. Ginger carried in a tray of cookies and handed them to Rowan. John ran over and grabbed Gracie's hand, leading her out to the backyard to play. They were good playmates.

"I missed you!" Giselle shouted.

I laughed. "I missed you, too. What's it been, like, six months since you came home? Is Florida that good, or have you been avoiding us? Where's Omar?"

She blushed. "Omar's at work. He's been doing lots of overtime in the ER. It's long hours. We've been so busy, and well, I have a surprise. I'm pregnant!"

Ginger's jaw dropped in shock. "What?!"

Giselle smiled. "I'm three months along. We're both excited. Omar is out of his mind. We're still thinking about names, but I want to name him Henry."

"It's a boy? That's...that's amazing," Ginger said.

Athena smiled. "Your baby boy will be so close in age to Ari. It'll be so fun!"

"I hadn't even thought of that," Giselle said, "we can give them matching outfits!"

They both laughed, and Giselle went over to see Ari. She looked down at his little face, probably imagining what her own baby was going to look like. I was unbelievably happy. This would be her first child. I already knew she and Omar would be phenomenal parents. They were both unbelievably kind and loving people. Their baby would be lucky.

Silently, Ginger tapped on my shoulder and motioned to the stairs. I nodded, slipping out of the room and following her. She walked up to the nursery and closed the door after I followed her in. There was sadness on her face. Considering that her twin sister had just announced her pregnancy, I had expected more excitement. Ginger and Giselle were as close as ever; they were practically inseparable. They shared happiness between the two of them, almost mirroring each other's emotions.

I took her hands in mine. "Ginger, what is it? Is something wrong?"

She lost all control and started sobbing. I wrapped her in my arms and held tight. Ginger rarely ever broke down. She was determined and strong. For a long time, she had suffered from infertility. But after she and Drew had adopted Gracie, she had never talked about having a biological child. I had assumed that they were planning to be a family of three. Maybe I had been wrong, though. Ginger had never mentioned losing a baby, but maybe there was something I didn't know.

I knew from experience that miscarriage hurt. Before conceiving John and Mina, I had lost my first baby. It had been devastating to Rowan and me. We hadn't even reached the second trimester, but losing our child had still been horrible. I still thought of that baby. Though we had never officially discovered the gender, I knew in my heart it had been a girl. Rowan and I had named her Rae. When I thought of our family, I included her. She was important to me.

Ginger sniffled and wiped her nose with a tissue. "I…I was waiting to tell everyone. I wasn't sure if I should say anything…the doctor told me it was better to wait to make the announcement. Drew wanted to tell you, but I was so scared. Last month, I—I lost two babies."

My breath caught in my throat. "Oh, Ginger, I am so, so sorry. I know how bad it hurts, I do. This must be terrible for you. Is there anything I can do to help?"

She looked up at me with tears in her eyes. "I just—I just don't know what to do. Giselle is so happy. I can't ruin that. And I don't want anyone to think I'm not thankful for Gracie—I am. I'm lucky to have a daughter."

"Shh," I whispered, "no one would

ever think you don't love Gracie. It's okay, I understand. I've been there, Ginger. I know it hurts more than anything in the world. Losing a baby, no less two, is horrific. It made me feel so guilty, and I know you must feel that way, too."

She nodded. "I was fourteen weeks along. After a few months, I was so certain. I thought it would be okay. We found out the twins were girls, and I couldn't wait to tell Giselle. I thought they would be just like us. But then, I went to the doctor, and the heartbeats were gone. I wanted to die, Lily, I really did."

I pulled her close. "Oh, Ginger, I wish I could tell you how sorry I am. I just don't know what to say."

She leaned against me. "I can't tell Giselle. She would feel bad about celebrating her baby if I told her. They would have been born so close together.

Mom would have had three new grandchildren in one year. Everyone would have been so happy. Now, I just sit and stare at the ultrasound photos, wondering how I'm going to keep going. Gracie has been the only thing motivating me."

"Did you name your girls?" I asked.

She nodded. "Liv and Lucia. I have the ultrasound pictures on my phone."

"Can I see them?" I whispered.

Ginger handed me her phone. I remembered how John and Mina had looked at that age, curled up inside my womb. Twins were such a beautiful thing. They had a bond like no other. It seemed that twins were common in Rowan, Ginger, and Giselle's family. But Ginger had lost her set, and she would never get them back. There was no way to comfort her.

"They're beautiful," I said.

She gave me a sad smile. "Thank you. We had a private funeral. I had no idea how to tell Gracie. She's still so little. We wanted you all to know, but I just didn't know what to say to her. She doesn't know her ABCs, no less anything about babies. I just didn't know how to tell my daughter her little sisters had died inside me."

I nodded. "I understand. Maybe you should talk to Athena."

Athena had lost her first son, Phoenix, when she was twenty weeks pregnant. It had been a horrible, bloody ordeal. No one liked to remember it. But she, better than most, understood what it was like to lose a child. She had labored for hours, only to be able to hold her deceased baby for a little while. It had been excruciating.

"Okay, but I don't know how to tell her," Ginger mumbled.

"Don't worry," I said, "I'll talk to her for you."

Chapter Fourteen
PRIVATE

"Hey, what's wrong?" Rowan asked.

I was brushing my hair before bed, staring in the mirror with a monotone expression. All I could think about was Beth in her bassinet, sleeping peacefully beside our bed. Ever since returning from the hospital, she had been in perfect health. She was happy, energetic, and eating well. I couldn't have asked for more.

Ginger was on my mind, though. I knew she was happy for Giselle, but I also understood her grief. I had arranged for her to go out with Athena to lunch tomorrow. It would be better for them to talk in private. Maybe they would be able to bond over their lost babies or at least sympathize with each other. I was just at a loss as to what to do.

"I need to tell you something," I said.

He nodded and sat down on his side of the bed. "What's going on?"

Luckily, John and Mina were asleep in bed. This needed to be a very private conversation. Giselle couldn't know. I understood why Ginger wanted to keep it private. If Giselle knew, she wouldn't be able to be happy about her own pregnancy. It made sense. Still, it was hard keeping secrets. In our family, everyone knew everything. With the exception of Drew, Ginger's husband, we were all supernatural beings. Faeries kept their secret from the world. We were good at leaving words unsaid and only telling others what was necessary. But within our own circles, it was the opposite. We lived in a community with lots of other faerie families. Everyone was close and cared about each other.

"You have to keep it a secret," I said.

"Okay," he replied, "from who?"

I took a deep breath. "Ginger doesn't want Giselle to know."

Rowan looked at me with surprise. "But she told you?"

I nodded. "It's sensitive. She didn't seem to know what else to do. I understand her perspective. All things considered, she's being very thoughtful."

Rowan seemed impatient. "So what is it?"

"Ginger was carrying twin girls. She lost them last month," I said.

We stared at each other for a moment. I had honestly started to believe that Ginger was unable to have children. She had been married to Drew for years, and there had never been any hint of a conception. We had never expected this.

"She…she miscarried?" Rowan whispered.

I nodded. "She just told me today."

Rowan closed his eyes. "Oh no, she must be feeling terrible. I'm sure she's happy for Giselle, but…"

"I know," I replied. "Ginger is having lunch with Athena tomorrow. I thought it would be good for both of them.

Rowan nodded. "That's a good idea. Maybe it'll help her."

I sighed. "I hope so. I wish I could do more, but it's all so complicated."

"We just can't ruin things for Giselle," he said.

I nodded. "I know."

We both lay down and pulled the

covers over us. It was warm and cozy. Our bed was the one place I felt we could have real conversations without anyone listening. Rowan turned on his side to switch the lamp off and then rolled over to look at me. He wrapped his arm around my waist and tucked my head against his shoulder. I breathed in his scent, remembering that with him, I would always be loved. He began stroking my hair and gently pulling the strands apart with his fingers.

"You're thinking about Rae, aren't you?" I murmured.

He paused. "Yes, I can't help it. I always knew I wanted children with you, Lily. When we lost our first baby, I thought it was all over. I was so thankful for the twins and then for Beth. Then, when Marie called us, I truly thought I was going to die. I didn't think I could handle losing another child, especially not one we had nurtured and loved beyond comprehension for a full year. Ginger and Drew must be miserable."

I cuddled closer against him. "I'll try to think of a way to help her."

He kissed my forehead. "Just another one of the many reasons I love you, Lily. You care so much."

I closed my eyes and began to drift off to sleep. "I try my best."

He nuzzled his head against mine. "I know."

Chapter Fifteen
GIVE ME TIME

The next day, I received an unexpected knock at my door. When I opened it, a smile spread across my face. It was my biological grandma, with her gray hair piled high and a smile full of energy. She still looked so young for her age. Maybe it was her smile, but there was something that gave her a sense of eternal youth.

"Grandma?" I asked.

She pulled me in for a long hug. "You didn't think I'd stay away, did you? My great-granddaughter had open-heart surgery. I wasn't about to keep to myself."

I watched as she walked in and set her bags on the floor. "But, grandma, I thought you were sick? You sent me an email last week saying your cancer was back again. I didn't want you to be too stressed."

She rolled her eyes. "My great-granddaughter is more important than keeping myself stress-free. Where is she?"

I motioned to the kitchen where Rowan was making lunch. Grandma strolled in, and John and Mina ran into her arms. I watched as she squeezed them both tight.

She smiled at them. "How are you two? You're getting so tall!"

"Will you play with us?" John asked.

"Yeah!" Mina said. "Daddy got me a new dollhouse. We can play in my room!"

"Just one minute, you two," Grandma said, "I need to talk to your father."

They both frowned but went back to eating their peanut butter and jelly sandwiches.

Rowan smiled at her. "Grandma, I didn't know you were coming. What about chemo?"

She shook her head. "You know I don't like human doctors. They make me suspicious. All their technology gives me a headache."

"Grandma," Rowan said, "human doctors have already given you five extra years. If you just keep doing your treatments, you'll live longer."

She pursed her lips. "Right now, I want to hold my youngest great-granddaughter."

Rowan sighed, and handed over the baby.

Grandma smiled. "There, much better."

Beth immediately started reaching for her dangly earrings, pulling on the gold flowers like they were toys. She tugged on them, but Grandma just laughed. They had always had a good connection. Grandma loved babies, and she was always happy for more time with her great-grandchildren. But she lived a good bit away, so she only came over about once a month. Her time with them was precious. She had ovarian cancer, and we weren't sure how much time she had left.

Grandma headed for the stairs with Beth in her arms. John and Mina dashed over to follow her. "Well, I'm going to play with the children. You two have fun."

Before I had the chance to say another word, my phone rang. Athena's name popped up on my screen.

"Hey, what's up?" I asked.

She sighed. "I just left the restaurant. You're right. Ginger is in bad shape."

"I know," I said, "what did you tell her?"

"I tried to convince her that Giselle wouldn't want her to keep it a secret, but she wouldn't listen. Ginger is determined to keep Giselle out of it," she said.

I bit my lip. "I just don't know what's the right choice, Athena."

"Neither do I," she murmured. "Giselle being pregnant sure complicates things."

I sighed. "I know."

"Well, let me know if you think of anything," she said.

"Okay, I will," I replied.

Then, it hit me. Doctor Lett could help. I was due back for my appointment with her, anyway. The medicine she had given me was amazing. Doctor Lett had acknowledged my depression and helped me to improve. I still didn't feel perfect, but that was okay. My life didn't need to be flawless. As long as I could function, love my husband, and take care of my children, then it was alright. Doctor Lett had helped me realize I needed help. Without her, I would still be in the same dark place. Maybe she could help Ginger, too.

"Rowan, I have an idea!" I said.

"What is it?" he asked.

I grabbed my purse and dashed out the door. "I'll tell you later."

"Well, okay," he said.

I unlocked my car, hopped in, and began the short drive to Ginger and Drew's house. Drew never worked on Fridays. I could take Ginger to see Doctor Lett right now. When I pulled into their driveway, I hurried past the marigolds to the front door. I rang the doorbell and waited for Ginger to answer.

"Lily?" Ginger said as she opened the door to let me in.

"Hey," I said, "I have an idea."

"What is it?" she asked.

I smiled. "Well, you know the reason Rowan and I went on the trip to Maine. The doctor who diagnosed me with Postpartum Depression really helped me see the light. She gave me some helpful meds, and I'm really starting to feel better about everything again. Maybe she could help you."

Ginger gave me a sad smile and pulled me over to her living room to sit down. It was a calm, peaceful place. There was a diffuser filling the room with the scent of lavender and two comforting candles burning. The couch and two chairs were both light gray, and the carpet was a soft cream color. The only bright things in the room were their most recent family photos. A large, framed picture of Gracie in a puffy pink dress hung right in the middle of the main wall, with pictures of the three of them on both sides. Ginger looked so happy in those. Her smile was real. I missed the light that had once been in her eyes.

"Lily," she said, "I've been on antidepressants for two years. After my miscarriage, my doctor upped my dosage. I know I have issues, but I'm doing the best I can. There's nothing else to try. I truly appreciate your idea. I do. It was very thoughtful of you, but it's just not the answer. Thank you, though."

I slumped back against the couch. I had gotten my hopes up too easily. It was never so simple. Maybe there really was nothing to do.

Ginger smiled at me. "Don't worry, Lily, I'll be fine. I'm in therapy, and it's helping. But the real key is time. Eventually, I'll be okay. Sometimes there's just no fast fix to these types of problems."

"Are you sure?" I asked.

She nodded. "Positive. Sometimes, all we can do is wait. Life has a habit of throwing things at us that we can't always handle. You know that. Just give me a little bit longer."

I pulled her into a hug. "You know I love you, right?"

"Of course," she said, "I love you, too."

Chapter Sixteen
NEVER FORGET

Beth really did have the prettiest eyes of any baby in the world. She looked up at me as I sat in the rocking chair. Beth gently sucked on her bottle, holding it up all on her own. Her blue eyes shone with the innocence of childhood. Soon, she would be playing with her siblings, running around, and eating real food. Part of me was excited, but I was also afraid of missing this. I didn't intend to have another baby. When Beth grew out of this phase, I would never have another infant of my own.

I barely noticed when Grandma

walked into the nursery. She stood in the doorway, leaning on the wall. I looked up at her, realizing just how tired she really was. Yes, she still had the same brightness as always. She had played with the twins all day and never paused to take a moment for herself. But she was also very sick, even if she wanted to hide it. There were dark circles under her eyes, and she walked with heavy shoulders.

"How are you, Lily?" she asked.

I looked at her curiously. "I'm fine, Grandma. How are you?"

She waved her hand. "We're talking about you right now. Don't spend your energy on me. You've got children to worry about."

"I'm okay, Grandma. I promise," I said.

"Lily," she replied, "Rowan told me everything."

"Oh," I said.

She grinned. "Yes, and I've been wanting to talk to you all day. Now that the twins are asleep, I have my opportunity. I want to know if you're doing any better. How are you feeling about motherhood, about all of it?"

I took a deep breath. "That's a big question. I'm not sure there's a simple answer."

She smiled. "It's a lot, but I want you to tell me all of it."

I nodded. "After having Beth, I never really bonded with her. I was lonely and sick of never seeing Rowan. Life seemed like one endless cycle full of changing diapers and making bottles. I was really starting to hate all of it. I wasn't eating, but I didn't want to acknowledge the problem. The medicine has really helped me."

"I'm glad, Lily," she said. "You're so young, and sometimes I worry you were burdened with too much too quickly. From the very beginning, your life was surrounded by complications. Fate hasn't been easy on you. But you are strong, I know that."

I smiled. "Things have changed. I spent a little time alone with Rowan, and that was heavenly. It felt like falling in love all over again. But when I thought I was going to lose Beth, my whole worldview shifted. Yes, the medicine had already started to work. It was a huge help. But the moment I heard my daughter had stopped breathing, my maternal instincts came out in full force. Suddenly, all I wanted to do was hold Beth and keep her safe. When I saw her for the first time after arriving, it was like watching her be born all over again. So much new love burst from my chest. I felt a true connection to her. Now everything has changed. I'm so happy to be her mother and so thankful that she's alive. If she had died, I don't know what I would have done. I love her so much."

Grandma walked over and placed her hand on mine. "You've always been a good mother, Lily. From the moment I saw you hold John and Mina, I knew you were meant to have children. You had a little bump in the road, but now you're on the other side. I have every confidence that you will continue to be the best mother for all three of your children. They'll grow up to be incredible individuals, just like you and their father."

She made me teary-eyed. "Thank you, that means so much."

Grandma smiled. "You deserve it, sweetheart."

Rowan walked up to the door. "Am I interrupting something?"

Grandma shook her head. "Not at all. I'm just checking to make sure you're treating my granddaughter right. I have to keep you on your toes."

He smiled. "Yes, ma'am. I'm doing my best."

She gave him a playful grin and walked out of the room.

"Want me to take her?" Rowan asked.

I shook my head. "That's okay, I'll stay for a while longer."

He stared into my eyes lovingly. "Well, if you get tired, I can take the night shift."

I smiled. "She's almost finished eating. I'm sure she'll go to sleep soon."

Rowan walked over and gave Beth a kiss on the top of her head. "Goodnight, baby girl." He leaned up to plant a gentle kiss on my lips. "I'll see you later, Momma."

He walked toward the door and winked at me as he started down the hall.

I sat with Beth for a while longer. Tonight was the first night we were going to try to put her in her crib. There were video monitors on both sides, so if anything went wrong, they would alert us. I was a little nervous, but we needed to try. I trusted that she would be alright.

When she had finally fallen asleep, I kissed both of her cheeks and took her bottle away. Beth breathed softly, peacefully sleeping in the blissful baby way. I nuzzled her close to my chest, breathing in her sweet scent. She still smelled like a baby, such a special thing. I placed her softly in her crib and looked down at her once again. Beth was my beautiful baby, and I would never forget it.

Chapter Seventeen
DO IT...AGAIN

"Which one are you thinking?" Giselle asked.

It was only a renewal of vows, not a full wedding. I wasn't sure why everyone was making such a big deal out of it. Rowan had already given me a beautiful ring. There wasn't a need for anything else. But since Giselle was back in town, she was insisting on going big or going home. And she definitely wasn't planning on letting me go home.

She had demanded we go wedding dress shopping. I couldn't believe that, after so many years, I was doing this again. It wasn't very thrilling to try on an endless number of dresses, but Rowan had also wanted me to go. He thought it would be a good way for Ginger, Giselle, and me to spend time together. After all, we had done this together before.

Giselle had hauled Ginger and me to another fancy wedding dress store. There was white all around us and crystal chandeliers hanging from the ceilings and the walls. Comfy couches and chairs were scattered in every corner, and there was an endless supply of dresses, shoes, and veils. I hardly knew what to say.

"Well, I don't know, Giselle," I said. "They all seem…a little extravagant."

Each dress she picked out was huge. They were practically overflowing with lace and had more glitter than I had ever imagined seeing. It was the second time around, and I wasn't interested in wearing a big dress again.

She raised her eyebrows. "What do you mean? These all cost half as much as your first wedding dress. They're not that expensive."

"I don't mean that," I said, "they're just a bit...poofy."

Ginger couldn't help but laugh.

Giselle shot her an angry glance. "What's wrong with poofy?"

Ginger shrugged. "Well, it isn't their first wedding. She had a huge dress then."

"Exactly," I agreed, "a smaller dress would be good."

Giselle rolled her eyes. "Fine, if you must."

I nodded. "Yes, I must."

Ginger laughed. "I'll go pull some smaller styles."

Several minutes later, Ginger brought back about fifteen different dresses. I tried all of them on, but Giselle was only happy with two of the options. The first was a plain satin gown with long sleeves and no details. It was elegant but not over the top. The dress could have passed for an evening gown if it was in a different color. The second one was knee-length and made of a soft cotton fabric. It was plain white with a regency waist and ruffled ends.

"I like the second one," I said.

Ginger nodded. "I do, too."

Giselle sighed. "Alright, but I get to pick the shoes."

My eyes grew wide. "Oh no, you don't."

Before I could stop her, she shoved a pair of white velvet heels into my hands. I looked at them in horror but was silent as she pushed me back into the dressing room. There was no response to give.

Reluctantly, I slid them on. They were uncomfortable, and I was afraid of falling. But to appease Giselle, who had at least relented on the dress front, I would wear them.

I stepped back out of the dressing room. "Fine, I'll wear them."

Giselle squealed with excitement. "Yay! Finally!"

Ginger grinned. "You're going to fall and break a leg."

I rolled my eyes. "Yeah, well, I guess I'll just have to blame her then."

Giselle shrugged. "It's all for the pictures. If you fall afterwards, no one will remember."

Ginger smirked. "Oh, I'm sure they'll all remember."

I threw a piece of silk at them. "Oh, stop it!"

We all laughed, and suddenly, I remembered a time, long, long ago.

Chapter Eighteen
PLEASE

It had been four weeks since Beth's open-heart surgery. She was doing much better and almost completely back to normal. Every morning, we gave her the pills prescribed by the doctor, but other than that, life went on. Beth had so much more energy and was sleeping through the night. She had become a happy baby.

My grandma had decided to sell her house and move into a small apartment near us. She wanted to spend more time with her great-grandchildren. Honestly, I thought that was only part of her motivation. She still eyed me carefully, even after our heart-to-heart conversation. I knew she wanted to help me with the kids to make life a little easier. She had nowhere else to be other than her chemo appointments I had finally convinced her to go to.

My parents had flown back to Florida, so Rowan was once again managing the store. He was still gone a lot, but not as much as before. We had hired a part-time employee to make things less stressful. Rowan was now only working until five every day instead of eight. It definitely made the evenings more pleasant.

Giselle had flown back home for a few weeks and then returned. She was determined not to miss our vow renewal ceremony. Her husband, Omar, was still occupied at work. He was the best kind of doctor, a dedicated one. Even though she had come back alone, with a newly developed bulge in the lower half of her stomach, she was making a splash. I had urged her not to, but Giselle had already ordered flowers, organized the food, and selected a cake. Ever since picking out my dress, I hadn't done anything to help the process. Giselle was the ringleader, and I was okay with that.

Ginger hadn't spoken to me about her miscarriage since our last conversation. She was being distant and spending most of her time with her husband and daughter. I certainly didn't blame her. Whether or not she got pregnant again, she would be in pain for a long time. I wanted to help her, but there didn't seem like much to do.

Tomorrow, I was going to renew my vows to my husband. Rowan was almost more enthusiastic than me. He had even taken more time than me to ask Giselle about the arrangements. I wasn't surprised, though. He was a truly good man. I had known that since the day I met him. Rowan had captured my heart from the very beginning, and I was prepared to renew my vows to him without a second thought. He had my heart, and that would always be the case. I had no reservations whatsoever.

As I was moisturizing my face in the master bathroom, Rowan came up behind me. "You excited for tomorrow?"

"Mmm," I replied, "well, I'm not as nervous as the first time. I'm surprised Giselle didn't haul you out of here. I expected her to say we couldn't spend the night with each other."

Rowan laughed. "She cornered me first. I refused."

I rolled my eyes. "I'm sure she didn't take that well."

He smirked. "I thought she was going to throw something at me."

"Well, I'm glad you're here," I said.

He nuzzled his face against my neck. "Me too, baby. I can't imagine spending the night away from you."

"I'm glad we haven't had to do it so far," I said.

He kissed me. "I'll try my best to make sure we never have to."

I leaned back against him. "How would you feel about having another baby?"

His jaw dropped. "What?"

I looked into his eyes. "Do you want another baby? When we first started dating, you told me you wanted a lot of them. Three isn't exactly a lot. Maybe just one more."

Rowan stood in silence. "Lily, you lost yourself for a full year after having Beth. The only reason you're finally starting to feel normal now is the shock of Beth having heart problems and medication. I'm not sure you're thinking clearly."

I pursed my lips. "Rowan, I am thinking clearly. Grandma is here all the time helping with the kids, and you're working less. It's easier now. If I had never developed Postpartum Depression, what would you say?"

The look in his eyes told me all I needed to know. If it were up to him, he would never want to stop having babies. He adored children. Money wasn't a problem, and our house was plenty big enough. My pregnancies were problem-free and didn't have long-lasting negative effects on my body. I already knew that having Postpartum Depression once didn't mean I would have it again. The medicine was really helping me. I felt fine. Better than fine, actually. I was really starting to enjoy life again.

"How about we talk about this

over the trip?" he asked.

After the vow renewal, Rowan and I were taking a brief, three-day trip to The Berkshires in New England. We were going to stay in a small lodge and spend some time outside, enjoying nature. I was looking forward to it. Grandma was going to stay at our house and take care of the kids. We had tried to convince her to let Marie keep them, but she was adamant. Grandma wanted to take care of her great-grandchildren. I couldn't really object.

"This isn't an excuse to get me to forget about it, is it?" I asked.

A guilty look crossed Rowan's face. "No."

"Don't lie to me," I said.

He sighed. "Maybe your hormones are making you feel weird."

I shook my head. "Rowan, I'm twenty-five. I'm not ready to leave the baby phase yet. I'm already feeling sad about moving away from breastfeeding. I want another baby."

"I'll…think about it," he said.

I nodded. "Good."

Chapter Nineteen
ROMEO

"Are you ready?" Giselle asked.

I looked down at my pretty white dress, terrifying heels, and a small bouquet of wildflowers. My hair was curled lightly and fell down around me in gentle waves. Giselle had spent hours on my makeup, making sure I looked perfect.

I smiled. "Yes, I'm more than ready."

It was a small crowd, just our close family and friends. I hadn't wanted a big production. Yes, it mattered to me, but this was more about my relationship with Rowan than anything else. This was for the two of us. It was nice having the support of our family, but ultimately, what mattered was renewing our vows.

We were in the beautiful meadow behind our house. It was brimming with new flowers that seemed even more vibrant in the sunlight. Everyone wore casual attire, summer dresses and shorts. John and Mina were more interested in playing and running around with Gracie and Luca than anything else. It was completely relaxed. People were drinking lemonade, snacking on fruit and cheese, eating sandwiches, and laughing with each other. I was comfortable. Ginger was going to perform the ceremony. She had a smile on her face, and it wasn't fake. I was glad she was feeling okay, even though I knew there was a part of herself mourning her twin girls every moment of every day.

Rowan stood beside me in khaki shorts and polo shirt. He had asked me if I wanted him to wear a suit, but I'd said no. My dress wasn't too fancy, and we were just going to relax. There was no reason for him to be uncomfortable around friends and family.

Grandma watched with a satisfied smile on her face as she sat a distance away, feeding Beth small slices of pineapple. It was Beth's new favorite food. She was content wearing a little pink sundress and happily eating. I smiled back at them and gave a little wave.

Rowan took my hand and pulled me in for a small kiss. Giselle didn't even protest. She smiled softly and rubbed her pregnant belly. I looked down at her stomach with a little envy, hoping Rowan would agree to my request.

"Hey!" Ginger shouted. "Everybody quiet down. We're ready to start."

The children continued to play, but I didn't mind. The adults settled down on the blankets surrounding us, and all smiled patiently. I glanced at Athena with her still-small newborn in her arms. She gave me a knowing look, and we both smiled. There would always be something unique between us.

"Well, since this is pretty informal, I'll let you two do most of the talking," Ginger said.

Rowan nodded and pulled a small gold band from his pocket. It matched the new emerald ring I had on my right hand. Now, I would have two sets of wedding bands. I didn't mind. It just showed how incredibly in love I was with my soulmate. He was my husband, and I couldn't have been happier about it.

"Lily," he said, "you already know

I love you. There's no one else I would rather spend the rest of forever with. You fill my life with laughter, smiles, and so, so much love. You've already given me three beautiful children, and I couldn't be more thankful to you for that. I can't even describe how much I adore you. After so many years together, I still look forward to seeing you every night. When I'm away, my thoughts are consumed with your beautiful emerald eyes and gentle smile. I truly wouldn't be able to survive without you. You're the best part of my life, and I couldn't bear losing you. I hope you know that I will never stop loving you. So today, I promise to continue providing for you, working to make you happy, caring for all of your needs, showing you affection and love, and never, ever give up on this marriage. You are my life, and I mean that with all of my heart and soul. I love you so much,

Lily."

He slipped the new ring onto my finger as tears fell from my eyes. I knew my makeup was running, but I didn't care. Giselle could worry about that. Rowan was everything I'd ever wanted. He knew that I needed reassurance and constant affection. And the best part was he had no problem giving me all the love I needed.

I looked up directly into his affectionate eyes. "Rowan, I have no idea what I would do or how I would live without you. You brought meaning into my life, and I know I could never have loved anyone the way I love you. It's hard for me to tell you how much I adore each and every aspect of your being. There's no part of my heart that doesn't belong to you because you're the man I always wanted. I'm even more in love than I was when we first fell for each other, and I'm thankful for our family and the happiness we have. I promise that none of that will ever change. Our wedding day feels like yesterday, and I have just as much passion for you now as I did all those years ago. We've gone through so much together and made it past what feels like endless challenges. But because of you, I've always known everything would be alright. No matter who or what tries to break us, I know they won't win. I will love you forever, Rowan, I promise."

I wasn't the only one crying. Grandma was practically sobbing and wiping her tears away with a handkerchief. Giselle, with her pregnancy hormones, was a mess, crying into Drew's shoulder. Athena was crying quietly, softly dabbing her tears away. Everyone else looked emotional, sentimental, and happy.

Rowan's beautiful brown eyes

were filled with love. When I looked up at him, I still saw the man I'd met my senior year of high school. I remembered him carrying me in his arms, laughing with me, kissing me, dancing with me, opening up to me, and sharing with me everything that mattered to him. When I looked at my husband, I saw the man I knew I would spend the rest of my life with. He was my confidant, the father of my children, my soulmate, and my best friend. There was nothing more I could want in a partner.

Ginger smiled at Rowan. "Well, I guess you should probably kiss your wife."

Everyone laughed, and Rowan leaned in to give me a soft, loving kiss. When he pulled me into his arms, the whole world faded away. It was like we were the only two people in the universe. His lips consumed my thoughts and transported me to a place where there was nothing but our love. He made me forget all of my fear, anxiety, and sadness. Rowan was my saving grace and the best thing that had ever happened to me.

"I love you, Lily," he whispered.

I leaned in to give him another tender kiss. "I love you, too, so, so much."

Chapter Twenty
BARGAIN

I looked out at the lake from our little balcony, admiring the gentle flow of the waves as the wind blew against the cool water. The Berkshires had beautiful scenery. It was calm, almost therapeutic. I understood why Rowan had chosen it for our trip. Even the breeze seemed to wrap me in a layer of comfort. There was nothing stressful about the place.

Rowan wrapped his arms around my waist as I continued sipping my tea. I was still in my nightgown with my satin robe covering my body. My hair was messy, and I looked like a wreck.

But Rowan didn't care. He never did. That was one of the best parts about him. Rowan wasn't surface-level. He didn't place worth on appearance or beauty. No matter what, he always gave me the same loving looks, even if I was a mess. In my mind, he always seemed perfect.

It was our second day of the trip, and neither of us had mentioned having another baby. He was probably hoping I wouldn't bring it up. I knew he was scared, and I was too. But I wanted another baby, and I was determined to have one. Deep down, I knew he wanted another one too. Rowan loved children too much to say no. He was just worried about me, and it really was sweet. Even so, I was determined to change his mind. I knew it was what I wanted.

"So," I whispered, "have you thought about it?"

His body stiffened. "About what?"

"Rowan," I mumbled, "you know."

He sighed. "Yes, I have."

"And?" I asked.

"I think you should talk to that doctor you like, the one who gave you the medicine," he said. "It might be good for you."

"And if I talk to her?" I replied.

He took a moment to think about it. "If you talk to her, and she says it's alright, then we can have another baby. But, if she thinks it's not safe, then no. I'm not taking chances with you, Lily. There's no way I would intentionally put you at risk. If we were reckless, and I let my emotions take the lead, and something bad happened, I would never forgive myself. We will be careful about this, or we won't do it. That's the end of the discussion."

I turned around to look into his eyes. "You worry too much."

He shook his head. "No, you don't worry enough about your own health and safety. I don't want something bad to happen."

"Like what?" I asked.

He frowned. "I don't want you to…hurt yourself."

I paused. "Rowan, I wouldn't."

"Lily, no chance. That's the end of the discussion," he said.

He was just trying to be careful. I couldn't fault him for that. After all, he was my husband, and it was his job. I would talk to Doctor Lett, and I'd ask her what she thought. Hopefully, she would agree. If not, I didn't know what I would do. Rowan would never agree if the doctor said it wasn't a good idea.

"So if Doctor Lett says it's okay, we can try for another baby?" I asked.

He nodded. "If it's what you really want. I just have to make sure you're thinking about every detail. It might be hard on you. There's no way I can decide. I've clearly never been pregnant, so I have no idea what it's like."

I laughed, and he grinned. "Well, alright. I'll ask her, but you better hold up your end of the deal. No backing out."

Rowan rolled his eyes. "I'll hold up my end as long as you promise to do yours."

I nodded. "Agreed."

He smiled at me. "Lily, you never cease to surprise me. I might be on my deathbed, and you'll still say something I never expected."

I laughed. "At least it keeps life interesting."

He hugged me close. "It definitely does."

Chapter Twenty-One
YES

Doctor Lett's office was still as charming and relaxing as I remembered it to be. This time, Rowan was keeping the kids, so I didn't have to bring Beth with me. I wanted to have a real heart-to-heart with Laura. She needed to know that I was ready for another baby so I could get the go-ahead and tell Rowan.

I sat patiently in the waiting room until the nurse called my name. She took me back to the same room as my previous visit and asked me the normal questions. Then I waited alone for Doctor Lett, making sure I knew what to say to convince her.

"Lily!" she said as she opened the door. "How are you doing?"

I smiled. "Good, the medicine you gave me really helped."

She sat down across from me. "That's great to hear. Anything else going on?"

I recounted the story of my first trip with Rowan and Beth's surgery. She looked a little shocked when I told her about the whole incident, but she was very attentive. Laura waited for me to recount everything before speaking up.

"That all sounds extremely stressful," she said.

I nodded. "It was. I could barely believe everything that was going on. But then it felt like something inside me clicked. When I saw Beth for the first time after the surgery, all of the love and emotions my mind had been holding back flooded my brain. I felt connected to her the same way I do to my other children. Now that she's had the surgery, she's a much happier baby. She sleeps through the night and doesn't cry as much. I feel like I can breathe again."

Laura smiled. "That's wonderful. I'll probably keep you on the medicine for a little while longer, just to make sure everything is alright. But it sounds like you're really getting better. I'm so happy for you. Obviously, Beth's condition and surgery were terrifying for you and Rowan, but they did have a positive effect. Now your baby is healthy, and you seem to have risen back up out of your depression."

I nodded. "Yes, and Rowan is working fewer hours. It really helps. He comes home and makes dinner every night so I can have a little alone time. It's a big relief. I can finally have a few hours to focus on my mental health and take a shower in peace."

"I can imagine that's a help. It's important for you to take a little time to focus on you. You're a mother but also a person. It's essential that you remember that," she replied.

"I can definitely feel the difference. My grandma also just recently moved to the area. She comes over almost every day after John and Mina come home from school," I said. "It's nice to have some adult communication during the day."

She nodded. "That's definitely important. It sounds like your life is really improving. Your stress levels have lessened, and you're finally having a little time to yourself. It's also really good that you have more time to spend with your husband."

"There was something I wanted to talk to you about," I said.

Laura wrote a few notes down on her clipboard and then looked back up at me. "Sure, what is it?"

I took a long, deep breath. "I would like to have another baby."

She looked surprised for a moment, then smiled. "And you would like to know if it's a good idea?"

"Yes," I said, "Rowan will only let me have another one if you say yes. He's worried."

She nodded. "I see. This is a common problem. Often, the husband is more worried than the wife. It's touching and sweet but can be annoying. My answer for you is, as long as you've thought it through, yes. It's safe for you to have another baby. I can't promise you won't experience the same symptoms again, but if you keep a lookout for the signs, we can address them earlier. Ultimately, that shouldn't be a reason for you to decide against it. If you want another child, that's a decision only you and your husband can make. You have a good support system, especially with your grandmother in town, to help with the kids. Your financial situation isn't an issue, and you have the means to take care of them. It's all up to you. I have no objections."

I gave her a huge smile and almost squealed. "Thank you! It means a lot. I really do want another child. Now Rowan will agree, and we can move forward."

She nodded happily. "I'm glad you have such a hopeful outlook on life now. It's a real improvement from your previous state. You'll be just fine."

Unable to stop myself, I gave her a big hug. "Thank you."

She hugged me back. "Just doing my job."

Epilogue

One Year Later...

I stared at the ultrasound screen,
waiting for the nurse to tell Rowan and
me whether we were having a boy or a
girl. Being four months pregnant, I was
ready to find out the gender. Rowan had
eased into the idea of having another
child. Now that one was on the way, we
were both excited. Everyone was happy
for us, even Ginger. She hadn't conceived
again, but I was really hoping she would.

The ultrasound tech looked at the
screen in confusion. "They told you that
you're carrying a single?"

I shared a nervous look with

Rowan. "Yes, is something wrong?"

She took another look, staring at the screen. "Have you had multiples before?"

I nodded. "Yes, we have twins. A boy and a girl."

She smiled and clicked a few buttons, taking pictures. I watched in confusion, wondering what she meant. Then I looked at the screen and knew exactly what I was seeing. I couldn't believe I was four months pregnant and hadn't known. They told me there had only been one baby. But I had seen plenty of twin ultrasound pictures, and I knew what this was.

"You're having twins," she said.

Rowan looked like he might faint, and I laughed. Neither of us had expected to have another set of twins, especially since Doctor Lett had been sure there was only one heartbeat. I could barely believe what I was seeing. But there were two babies on the screen, curled up close and cuddling.

"Boys or girls?" I asked.

She smiled. "Well, I know how they missed it. It took me a minute, but there are definitely two babies. They're identical boys. One was probably behind the other during your first few scans."

I stared at the screen in shock. Identical boys? I had never ever expected that. It would be so different. No one in my family had identical twins. This would be a whole other challenge. But I was happy, that was for sure. Two more babies were going to join our family. No wonder my stomach was so big. I was attributing it to being my third pregnancy, but now I knew the truth. We were having twins again, and I couldn't wait. Rowan and I were going to have five children, a huge family. But I was excited, and I could tell from the glimmer in his eyes that he was, too.

"That's crazy," Rowan said.

I grinned. "Can you believe it? Identical boys."

He laughed. "I'm still shocked. It's going to take a little while. I guess we'll need some extra clothes. John is going to be so excited."

I looked back at the ultrasound screen, staring happily at my two babies. This wasn't what I had expected, but it was what I wanted. Rowan and I were going to have two more babies to love. Everyone would be so excited, especially Grandma. She had been declared cancer-free and in perfect health. I had no doubt that she would be with us for many more years.

"Congratulations," the ultrasound technician said, "you have two perfectly healthy baby boys. I'll print some pictures for you."

I felt silly for smiling so big, but I couldn't help myself. It was so perfect. Finally, I felt like our family was going to be complete. This time, I knew it was really going to be the beginning of our perfect little forever.

Five Months Later...

They were beautiful, so, so beautiful. Finally, I was holding my new set of twins. Rowan sat beside me, staring at them with a huge smile on his face. They were indeed very identical. Both boys had heads full of blond hair, the same as John, and bright blue eyes, just like Beth. They had golden skin that looked like Rowan's and pink lips the same as mine. To me, they were the most beautiful babies to ever be born. Along with my other children, of course. Even in the terrible hospital lighting and very uncomfortable bed, it all felt perfect. My baby boys were so peaceful, cuddling up against my chest and softly cooing.

"Mommy, can we see the babies?" Mina shouted as she ran into the room.

John was right behind her with a giddy smile on his face. When we had told him he was going to have two brothers, he had jumped with excitement for a whole month. John had always said he wanted a brother instead of a little sister. Well, now he had two.

"Sure, princess, Daddy can hold you up to look at them," I said.

Rowan picked her up and set her on his lap. She looked at the babies in awe, carefully reaching over to touch them. She was incredibly gentle, almost like she was afraid they might crumble and break. Mina was so soft-hearted. Sometimes, I worried she wouldn't survive in the world, but then I remembered her rambunctious brother. He would make sure she was safe. Grandma walked in carrying Beth on her hip, and Marie and Forest were right behind her. The happy great-grandma, aunt, and uncle all smiled. They were glowing with happiness. In the faerie world, babies were always a good thing. We already had a small population, and everyone loved seeing families grow. There was no such thing as too many babies. As Mother Teresa had said, "How can there be too many children? That is like saying there are too many flowers." Once, I hadn't thought that, but now I did. I couldn't imagine a world without all five of my babies. They were each precious. Without them, everything would be dull.

"What are their names?" John asked.

Rowan smiled and pulled him onto his lap beside Mina. "Finn and

Sawyer Marx. What do you think of your brothers?"

John jumped up and down. "Can I play with them?

Rowan laughed. "Maybe in a few months. They're too little to play now. We have to be careful with them. Remember how tiny Beth was when she was born."

John had a disappointed look on his face but nodded. They could play together soon enough. He was so energetic. I loved that about him, especially because he was so much like his father. One day, he would grow up to be exactly like Rowan. Grandma carried Beth over, and she looked curiously down at her brothers.

"Babies?" she asked.

Grandma nodded. "That's right, babies. Those are your brothers."

Beth wasn't exactly sure what that meant, but she clutched her baby doll and seemed to understand a little. She smiled brightly and kept looking down at the babies."

Giselle burst into the room with her husband, Omar, carrying their little boy, Henry, right behind her. "Let me see the babies!"

She rushed right toward me and stared down at them, "Aww, they're so cute. How adorable! I just wanna squeeze and cuddle them."

I smiled. "Trust me, I feel the same way."

A few moments later, the room was flooded with people. Ginger came in with her very pregnant belly sticking out in front of her. Drew was by her side, holding Gracie's hand. Ginger was having a baby girl. She was glowing with beauty and happiness. I was so excited for her. Everyone was.

"Aww," Ginger said, "they're

perfect."

Rowan smiled, still staring down at them. "Thank you, they definitely are."

Athena, Rhett, Jack, and LeAnne all came into the room together. Luca and Ari were with them, too. All of my favorite people were surrounding me. I smiled, so, so happy with the way things had turned out.

Jack gave me a knowing look, and I smiled. He mouthed, "They're beautiful," and moved to the back of the room to wait his turn.

Athena moved to stand beside me, and everyone stepped away to let her through. She reached down to touch Finn's hand and then moved on to Sawyer. Her face was filled with love.

"You have perfect babies, Lily. I'm so happy you finally have everything you want. You truly deserve it. You're an amazing mother, and I know they'll be loved," she said.

I felt my eyes fill with tears. "Thank you, Athena. That means a lot."

She smiled and squeezed my hand. "I'm always here for you."

I pulled her into a half hug. "I know."

My world was utterly perfect. Rowan and I had been through so much: we survived multiple murder attempts, had five children, and lived through medical crises, a miscarriage, my depression, and numerous other tragedies in our family. But now, it was peaceful. Yes, our house would be filled with the cries of two infants, and we would be up at night. Still, our family was whole and safe, and all of our children were healthy. My marriage was strong, and I had the best family I could ever want.

Rowan's eyes met mine, and we

both smiled. Yes, everything was turning out the way we wanted. We had our children and a happy life. It was like my love for him was blooming all over again. For a while, my heart had been like a flower during the winter, all wilting and dead. But now it was springing to life and more beautiful than ever before. I was unbelievably happy and more thankful than I could describe. My world was once again filled with light, but this time, it was here to stay. I was loved more than I had known possible, and I felt hope for the future. Everything felt perfect and truly complete. There was nothing more I desired, and that was the mark of a sincerely content, happy life. I was going to live each day filled with joy. And in that moment, looking around at my husband and all the people I loved, I knew that my story was really just beginning. This life was going to be exactly what I had always dreamed of, and I couldn't wait for it to continue to bloom.

Abby Farnsworth is the YA paranormal and urban fantasy romance author of the EverGreen Trilogy. Her books are targeted toward teens and young adults but can be enjoyed by readers of all ages.

She enjoys traveling, history, and reading a good book. When not working on her next novel, she can be found taking long walks exploring the natural world, trying a new recipe, or singing in various ensembles.

She currently resides in West Virginia with her family but adores trips to the beach, mountains, cities, and historical landmarks.

To learn more about Abby, her books, and current projects, take a look at the following:
#authorabbyfarnsworth
#theevergreentrilogy
Instagram: @abbyfarnsworth.writer
Facebook: @abbyfarnsworth.writer.poet

Made in the USA
Middletown, DE
29 October 2023

41381477R00120